Table of Contents

PREFACE

In this novel the writer is inspired to present to Urban readers a most realistic and self-related fiction story of the likes and lives of the Urban lifestyle.

The writer gives insight to some of the most troubling and life defeating obstacles for the majority of our Urban youth, who on a daily basis have to deal with the struggle of poverty, systematic oppression, and unexplained digressions as they progress through the early stages of their lives.

Also, to address the misunderstanding of the Urban life and to show how sometimes troubling circumstances can affect our youth in disturbing ways, and that not all youth are comfortable with them, but when placed in unfamiliar situations, they revert back to the only way they know and are comfortable with.

The everyday struggle for them is enough to cause any competent adult to question the meaning of right and wrong when dealing with dilemmas to survive. So, who are they to pass judgment or place blame on the victims for surviving the wicked ways of the Urban communities by the means they deem fit?

"A BORN VICTIM OF THE GAME"
PROLOGUE

"Aye, yo, guard, we need some help down here! It's an emergency!" yelled an inmate on the cellblock. "Girl, just stay calm and breathe slow."
"Aye, guard, come on man, she's going into labor down here!" she yelled again. Her cellmate's water just burst in the middle of the night. She continued to call out for help from the prison guards.
Even after all of the yelling and banging the inmates were doing, it still took several minutes for a guard to get on the cellblock.
"Damn man, what the hell was you doing? She's going into labor and you need to get her some fucking help!" yelled the inmate.
"Matthews, can you stand up for me?" asked the guard, looking through the six inch window on the cell's door, trying to analyze the situation.
"No I can't!" replied inmate Matthews laying in a puddle of her own birth fluids.
Matthews was serving time in 'Fluvanna Prison for Women' for prostitution and drug possession. She didn't have any steady or moral relationships. She just roamed the streets with a Love-Hate thing for heroin and crack. She was pregnant at the time of her

arrest and doesn't have a clue who the father is.

"Medical 10-18, Medical 10-18 on block C" reported the guard through his walkie-talkie. The jingle of keys and footsteps could be heard in the distance as help arrived within seconds of getting the call for a medical emergency. Prison guards and nurses rushed on the cellblock. "She's going into labor and says she can't stand up" spoke the guard to one of the nurses.
"We need to get her to the hospital ASAP!" replied the nurse. "Ms. Matthews, we're going to need you to stand and lay on this medical cart so we can quickly get you to medical, okay" she spoke calmly.
They got Matthews on the cart and began rushing her to the prison medical department. "She's not gone make it. Place her down right here, we need to do this now" spoke the nurse. "Matthews, we're going to do this now. Okay now, slowly take deep breaths and push as hard as you can."

Matthews lay there in the middle of a prison hallway crying in pain as she began giving birth.
After several minutes of pain and pushing, she finally gave birth. "Here it comes!" yelled the nurse.
Matthews passed out right after her last push

and was flown to Henrico Doctors Hospital by Medical Helicopter. She came to and found herself connected to medical equipment and handcuffed to the bed.

"CONGRATULATIONS, IT'S A BOY!" yelled the doctor holding up the newborn like a trophy.

"Oh my God! Can I hold him please?" asked Matthews.

The doctor looked in the direction of the prison guard. The guard just stood there and nodded his head in approval. The doctor carefully handed the baby to Matthews while she remained handcuffed to the bed.

"Aww, thank you so much! Look at my li'l man!" cried Matthews in-between sobs.

The doctor began explaining her health, but she wasn't hearing anything that he was saying. She clutched her newborn son tightly and held him close to her breast. She began crying tears of joy and fear, as thought of the lifestyle her son might live while having to grow up without a mother and a father flashed before her eyes.

Living at the bottom of this cold world for so long, has opened her eyes up to some of the most extreme circumstances. Now, bringing a boy into this world without a father or mother, has brought the worse feeling of fear possible.

CHAPTER ONE

Almost twelve years later, while enjoying his summer break before the start of sixth grade year.

"Aye Mah, can I?," spoke Malik, but his words were cut short by the sight of his aunt being lifted to another world by smoking crack.
"Damn it Malik! Didn't I tell your ass about running into my room without knocking? Shit, what you want?" asked his aunt while trying to hide her pipe thinking that he didn't see it.
"Mah, what are you doing?"
He referred to his aunt as his mother because she raised him while his real mother lived in and out of prison.
"I'm not doing anything! Now, what do you want?"
"No. What are you doing with all that?" He asked pointing to the big piece of coke, about the size of a Kit-Kat candy bar, that was on the bed.
"I'm minding my got-damn business! See I done told your ass about being nosey."
"But Mah, you know you're better than that."
"Boy, go on and get the hell up out my face. I'm grown and I do whatever I damn well please! Now, I'm already stressed about the rent for this month, so please don't make me take it

out on you."
"Well, let me help you" replied Malik looking more serious than 'The Rock' after saying his famous line.
"And how in the hell you think you gone help Malik?"
"Let me sell this for you" he spoke while holding the big piece of coke in his hand.
"Malik, go ahead and stop playing with me boy!" she yelled as she snatched the coke from his hand.
"But I know what I'm doing."
"And how the fuck you know what to do?"
"I've done it before" he replied, half lying because he never has sold crack before, but he's seen how it's done however; he had stayed in houses with his aunt and sisters without lights, water, and a lot of time no food. His aunt's oldest daughter and son used to work at the McDonald's on Mechanicsville Turnpike, and they used to steal food for the rest of the family to eat. They used to have to wait until their neighbors went to sleep. Just so they could steal their neighbor's waterhoses and fill up buckets of water to wash up with. Then, they would take the dirty buckets of water, remove the lid off the back of the toilet, and pour in the dirty buckets of water just to flush the toilet. So, he might not have sold crack before, but he was willing to try almost anything to be sure that he and his sisters didn't have to go through that again.

"Boy what am I going to do with you?" asked his aunt with her face buried in her hands in disbelief.
"Just let me help you Mah."

His aunt stared at him long and hard. She had accepted custody of Malik straight from the hospital the night he was born. She raised him by herself with her own 3 kids and his little sister. A single, middle age mom, a graduate from high school with a degree in nursing. Still she worked hard to be able to take care of her kids. She just had a problem with drinking and getting high in her leisure time, in hopes of escaping the stress.
'Damn! I don't need him telling people I get high, but what am I going to do?' she thought to herself.
Finally, she gave him a answer. "Okay. I'll let you help, but don't you tell nobody about none of this Malik, and I mean it!" She opened up the sandwich bag and broke a piece of the coke off for herself before handing the rest to Malik.
"I won't Mah, I promise" he said feeling like a kid in a candy aisle. Happy, he was ready to be a young coke-boy, like all the older niggas he hung around.

Malik was very mature and wise for an eleven year old. He rarely hung around kids his own age, but always stuck around the grown folks especially the hustlers. Although they wouldn't give him anything to sell, they let him smoke weed and paid him money for telling them when the law was coming.

Malik rode his Huffy bike down Phulpt Street, which is one of the drug strips in his neighborhood. He grew up in Fairfield Court Projects also known as Cashfield to the hustlers. Phulpt Street is a well-known strip all across the city.
Malik spotted Big Cee, one of the older hustlers Malik hung around. Big Cee's a heavy set, brown skin nigga. Weighing about 240 pounds, 5ft 11, with cornrows. For a fat boy, Big Cee dressed fly and was well known for getting that bread.

"Aye yo Cee, what's up bra?"
"Ain't none but a different day with the same ole shit. What's up with you li'l nigga?" Big Cee asked smiling like the Kool-Aid Man.
"Nothing. Trying to make me some money."
"Oh yeah! How you gone do that?"
"I got this." Malik reached inside his pocket and pulled out the work he had got from his aunt.
Big Cee looked at Malik in shock. Seeing an eleven year old kid pull out that much crack had caught him off guard. "Where the hell you get that from?"
"Look, I'm just trying to help my mama out with the rent."

Big Cee looked at Malik whose facial expression spoke, 'I'm serious'. "Aight, come with me li'l nigga."
Big Cee took Malik to this house he'd never been in before, where this dirty old dude with a natural smell of wine, piss, and cigarette smoke lived. It was a small, 1 bedroom project apartment.
As they entered the apartment, Malik instantly noticed that it was filled with roaches and empty beer cans scattered across the floor. An old brown leather couch sat up against the wall, facing the old school, floor model, color TV. They made their way to the kitchen and sat at the dirty, oak round table.
Big Cee broke a piece of the work that Malik had and gave it to the old dude. "Test this and tell me what you think about it."
With no hesitation, the old dude grabbed a metal spool out the sink. Then, he put a little bit of water in the spoon and put the piece of coke on the spoon. Next, he went and turned on one eye of the gas stove and placed the spoon on top of the fire for a couple of seconds.
Malik was about to witness how smoking coke was done for the first time.
The old dude scraped the coke from the spoon and placed it in his glass pipe. Then, he took a cigarette lighter, lit the pipe, and deeply inhaled at the same time. He started blowing out smoke and smacking his lips, like he was a

judge in a taste test. "Whoo boy, that's some good shit! I ain't have no coke like that in a long time. Wherever you get that from, you should keep getting it."

Malik sat at the table, 'How the fuck this nigga just stand right in front of me and get high like that?' He thought to himself as he watched the old dude continuously peek out the window, with his lips moving from side to side.
Big Cee stood and walked to the wooden cabinets and pulled out a plate, and a box cutter. "Now that we know this shit is good, you need to start cutting and bagging it up."
"I don't know how to cut up no work" replied Malik.
"Well, let me show you li'l nigga."
Malik sat and listened as Big Cee taught Bagging Up 101.
Big Cee took a box of sandwich bags off the top of the refrigerator. "Look, all you got to do is take the blade and cut the work into little pieces almost the size of red hots candy. Be careful and make sure that you hold the blade at an angle while you cut. Don't just have the blade straight down and cut because if you do, that's going to cause the coke to crumble up. And that's gone leave you with a lot of shake leftover when you're finished, and you don't want that. Now, after you've finished cutting all this shit up, put one piece in the corner of the bag and tie it up like this. Aight! You got

it?"
"Yeah, I got you bra."

Malik did exactly what Big Cee had showed him. He'd cut up all the block into little pieces, some bigger than the others. When he finished cutting he started bagging up and in about 30 minutes he was done. He had one hundred and forty unevenly cut pieces of crack that looked like bath salt.

Big Cee and Malik left the old dude's house and went back on Phulpt Street. They went to the Phulpt Street Apartments, which aren't big. It's a reddish-orange brick building in a L-shape that everybody called the Phulpt Street Apartments because no one knew its real name.
They stood there and waited for someone to come and buy some work. It was 4:50 in the afternoon and the sun was on its blaze. At a little after 5 o'clock the streets were flooded with all kinds of people looking to score their drug of choice.

"What's up auntie?"
The lady looked at young Malik, posted on the block like a lost child trying to hustle, and went straight to Big Cee. "What's up Cee, what you working with today?"
"I'm not doing anything today, but my li'l nigga got some popcorn for you though."

"Who is your li'l nigga, and where's he at?"
"He right there." Big Cee nodded towards Malik with a smile.
The lady looked in Malik's direction and was puzzled. "Who you talking about?; that li'l boy over there?"
"Yeah, just go holla at him."

"What's up auntie?" asked Malik.
"What you got li'l boy? And it better not be fake."
"Look, first off, my name's not li'l boy. Second of all, I wouldn't even sell you nothing that was fake, but I got whatever you want. I heard that its good. I wouldn't know because I don't do it."
She was shocked and couldn't help but to smile from the way Malik handled himself.
"Well okay li'l man, I'll try it out. So how much you gone give me for $20?"
"I'll give you 3 dimes for that money auntie."
"Aight, and it better be good too!"
Malik took the money, put it in his pocket, then gave the lady the work. He was happy and amazed at how fast and easy it was to make money.
Big Cee stood beside Malik with a big smile on his face. "Yeah my li'l nigga, that's how you do it!"
Malik smiled back at him. "Shid, I learned from watching y'all everyday."

With the help of Big Cee, Malik was hitting all kinds of sells: from $5 - $7 to $70 and $80 sells. At the end of the night, Malik had sold all of the work and made $993. At just eleven going on twelve years old, he couldn't believe how much money he'd just made.

"Damn Big Cee, I ain't never seen this much money before in my life bra! So how much do I owe you?"
"You don't owe me shit li'l nigga. Just make sure you give that bread to your mama so she can pay her rent."
"Aight, but good look for helping me. Real talk!"
"That's what Real Niggaz do. Now, don't you try and make this shit a habit tho'. Its more to this shit than making money. You could get locked up and taken away from your family, robbed, and killed behind this shit! So, don't try to start doing this shit until you're really ready for what come with it li'l nigga. Believe me, when them people get a nigga in that room and start talking about that time, even the hardest niggas start singing like 'Maxwell'. Never snitch, that's the GOLDEN RULE! Remember that."
Malik shook his head in disgust. "Shid bra, I ain't know it was that serious tho'."
"Yeah li'l nigga, it's a cold game. But after what I saw and how you handled everything today, when you get older and ready for the game

just let me know li'l nigga. Now go home, its already late, and holla at me tomorrow."
Malik and Big Cee shook hands.
"Aight bra, I'll catch you tomorrow" spoke Malik before walking off.
Big Cee just stood and watched Malik as he walked away. 'That young nigga got it. He's going to be something special for the streets when he gets older.' Big Cee smiled at his thoughts and walked off.

"KNOCK, KNOCK, KNOCK, KNOCK!"
"Who is it?" yelled Malik's li'l sister Jay.
"It's me!" yelled Malik.
"It's Malik Mah, and he know he's not supposed to be outside this late at night!" she yelled as she opened up the door.
"Shut up! You always trying to tell something." Malik slightly pushed her in the forehead and walked upstairs to his aunt's room. "Here Mah. I hope it's enough for the rent." Malik handed her the money he made. "It's everything that I made and I sold it all."
His aunt looked at him in disbelief. "Boy, how in the hell you get all this money, and don't you lie to me?"
"I sold the stuff you gave me. Ain't that's what I was supposed to do?"
"Yeah. Now, go eat and go to bed." She couldn't believe that Malik had sold all of that crack like that, and it kind of scared her too.

Malik lay in bed thinking about everything that Big Cee had told him could happen, but how fast and easy it was to make the money had giving him way more to think about.

CHAPTER TWO

A couple weeks later.

With the thoughts of school coming up and how fast it would be to make some money, Malik started looking for ways to get money so, he would be able to buy his own coke pack.

"Malik, your mentor is coming to pick you up at 3 o'clock so, make sure you be around" spoke his aunt.
"Aight. I ain't going nowhere but on Phulpt Street."
"Well, make sure you have your ass back here by 3 o'clock because don't nobody got time to be looking for you!"
Malik was irritated. "So what time is it now?"
"It's already 1:15, so you ain't got nothing but about a hour and a half to do whatever you gone do."
"I'm just gone go on the front with everybody else then."
Malik went out on the front and played 'throw it up and run' (a football game) until his mentor came to pick him up.

Malik continued to play football until he saw his mentor's car ride past, and he ran back to his house.
"Well, hey Malik, how are you doing?" asked

his mentor.

"I'm good, and you?" replied Malik as they both shook hands.

"I'm doing well Malik, thanks for asking. So, is your mother home so I can make sure that it's alright for us to leave?"

"Yeah, she's in the house. I'll go and get her. Aye Mah, my mentor is outside and he wants you."

"What the hell do he want? I don't feel like getting up right now Malik!"

"He wanna ask you, if I could leave with him?"

"Tell him 'yes' Malik, and leave me the hell alone please."

"She said that it's okay for us to leave, but she doesn't feel like being bothered right now. I guess she's got an attitude or something" spoke Malik shrugging his shoulders.

"Well Malik, what do you want to do today?"

"Let's go and do some work at your house."

Malik's mentor is a middle age English guy, retired from a lengthy career at DuPont. He has no kids with his wife of nearly twelve years so, he spent part of his spare time with Malik.

"I need some help painting the basements." He was talking about the two houses that he'd built from the ground up, right beside his home.

He would teach Malik how to do certain things and let him help out around the house to earn some money.

After helping his mentor paint both of the basements, they went back to his mentor's house for dinner. Malik chose to play on the laptop computer and look at all the latest Urban gear on Footlocker.com.
"I got to come up with a pack so I can get me some real money."
With that in mind, Malik stood and walked to the kitchen cabinets. He remembered that his mentor always kept a white envelope in the cabinet. He opened up the cabinet, grabbed the envelope, and took a handful of bills out.
Hearing his mentor coming down the stairs startled him, Malik tiptoed his way back to the computer as if he never moved.
"So Malik, what do you want to eat?
Malik loved being with his mentor because he introduced him to a better side of life. He took him to fancy restaurants with expensive foods. They went to a lot of different places like museums, the White House etc.. He also taught him a lot of lessons on life and becoming a man.
"Let's eat some steak."
Grilled steak, homemade mashed potatoes, steamed mixed vegetables and dinner rolls was the meal for dinner. After dinner his mentor took him back home.

When Malik got home, he walked to the

bathroom and counted the money that he'd just stolen from his mentor. When he finished counting he ended up with $340 in twenty dollar bills. In the midst of feeling happy and sad, happy because he finally had the money to buy his own coke pack, but sad because he'd stolen it from his mentor. Malik thought about what he was going to do with the money.

The next day, Malik rode his bike up Mechanicsville Turnpike to DTLR. He brought himself a pair of all black Air Force Ones and a pair of butter Timbs. He paid a sum of $197.78 for both pairs of shoes.
He made it back home while his sisters La-La and Jay was still outside playing, giving him time to put up his new shoes without anyone noticing them. He stashed the shoes in the back of the living room closet, where no one would look and see them.

Malik left the house and headed for Phulpt Street. When he reached Phulpt Street, he spotted Big Cee leaning inside of a car talking to someone.
"Aye, yo Cee! What's up up bra?" yelled Malik interrupting Big Cee's conversation.
Big Cee looked at the young nigga suspiciously, until he realized who it was. "Oh, my li'l nigga! What's up shawty, where the hell you been at these last few days?"
"I just been chilling. I gotta come up with some

back to school money."
"So what's up with yo mama? Don't she have you some shit for back to school?"
"Mane, you already know how it be. It ain't no telling what she's going to do. But look, I got $120 and I'm tryna get some bread. So, what's up?"
"Do you remember everything I told you last time?"
"Yeah, I remember and I'm ready now."
"Aight. Wait right here and I'll be right back." Big Ccc walked inside one of the apartments to get the coke for Malik. "Listen, this is 7 grams and all I want is for you to spend the money back with me. I'm not helping you this time. You're going to have to compete like the rest of us."
"That's a bet bra, I can do that."
Malik accepted the challenge and spent the rest of his day on the block hustling.

He woke up early just to get out and grind on Phulpt Street. Malik loved that feeling he got from hustling. It made him feel like a grown man, which he thought he was anyway.

At 10 o'clock in the morning, Malik was the only one standing out on Phulpt Street. He hollered at everyone who walked past and looked as if they got high.
"Aye unk! What's up, you aight?"
"Naw nephew, I ain't got no money right now.

So, lookout for me one time" replied the crack feign trying to get something free from the li'l nigga.

"Aight. I'll lookout for you, only if you lookout for me."

"What you need me to do baby boy? Come on, talk to me now nephew!"

"I need you to bring sells to me and I'll make sure your good for the day."

"How much you gone give me for all that?"

"I'll give you a twenty plus $5 for every 10 sells that you bring to me."

"Yeah nephew, we can work like that." Spoke the feign anxious to get his first fix of the day.

"Here." Malik gave the feign a $20 piece of crack and $5.

"Okay nephew. So, where you going to be at when I come back?"

"I'm gone be right here all day. I ain't going nowhere else."

"I'm gone make this quick so, make sure you be right here" spoke the feign in a rush to get his first blast.

Malik stood out on Phulpt Street, just him and his worker. They made all the money until, everybody else came out around 12 o'clock. At nearly 1 o'clock, the block was jumping. You had your weed man, coke boy, dope boy, and pill man. Even the bitches hustled from selling drugs, boosting, and setting a nigga up to get robbed.

Malik just sat and chilled while his worker brought money to him.
This became his daily routine.

CHAPTER THREE

While walking from his oldest sister's house on 23rd street. Malik turned around from the sound of someone calling his name.

"Aye Malik! Let me get a dollar. And I know you got one so, don't even try to lie!" yelled his li'l sister Jay rolling her neck like a bobblehead doll.
"Here." Malik reached in his pocket and pulled out a single dollar bill.
"Aight, now I can go to the candy lady."
"Ain't you suppose to say thank you or something?"
"Boy whatever! Thank you" she replied sarcastically.
"I want one too Malik!" yelled his youngest sister La-La as she began running from the porch.
Malik gave La-La two dollars. "Don't tell Jay."
"Thank you. I won't tell her but, that girl right there, she likes you."
"Which one?" asked Malik while looking at the girls on the porch.
"The one in the red shirt, standing beside Jay."
Malik noticed the light skin girl, with the ponytail, standing beside Jay. Wearing a red tank top, black Capri's, and a pair of red and black Jordan number nines. "Yeah I see her, but why didn't she come over here?"

"I told her to come over here and talk to you, but she act like she's scared or something."
"What are you and Jay doing over there anyway?" he asked after seeing people roam in and out of the house.
"The lady having a baby shower and said that we could come."
"Do you think she'll trip if I came over there?"
"I don't know, but she shouldn't. All you got to do is come over there with us."
"Aight, I'll be back in a minute."
"Where you about to go?"
"I got to go around the street real quick and I'm coming right back." He spoke meaning every word because he was interested in talking to the light skin girl.

Malik walked behind the projects on Phulpt Street, to his li'l chill spot. He sat on someone's back porch and rolled up a blunt. After smoking half the blunt, he put the rest out and began walking back on 23rd street where his l'il sisters were.
"Aye Jay, come here real quick!" yelled Malik.
"Boy! What do you want now?"
"Where's the girl with the red shirt, that said she likes me?"
"She's in the house. Why, you want her?"
"Yeah. Tell her to come outside and y'all come sit on Michelle's porch with me."
"Boy! Why you just won't come and sit on this porch with us?"

"Cause, I don't know them people."
"So what. We don't know them either and they let us come over there!"
"Look, just go get yo'girl and come on Michelle's porch."
"Aight boy, with yo scared self!"

Malik walked three doors down and sat on his oldest sister Michelle's porch. He saw Jay come out the front door with the girl right behind her. He tried to lean back in his chair and pretended not to see them.
"Girl, come on and see my brother! And stop tryna act like you shy."
"Girl naw! Ain't nobody acting shy" screamed the girl wearing the red shirt.
"Here she go bra!" yelled Jay all extra loud and excited.
Malik took a good look at her face. "So, what's up with you? What's your name?"
"Hey, I'm Keisha" replied shyly by the girl wearing the red shirt.
"Keisha! Why they name you that?"
"Lord have mercy! Why is you asking her all that for?" butted Jay.
"'Cause I want to! You need to mind your business."
"Well then, next time don't ask me to do nothing for you. With yo whack ass!"
Malik looked at Keisha while she laughed at him and Jay. "Don't laugh at her because she ain't even funny."

"Yes she is because she thinks she's somebody mamah."
"'Cause girl! His whack ass got the nerve to ask you, why they name you Keisha."
"Where you from shawty?"
"I'm from South Side. Why?" asked Keisha, with her hand posed on her hip.
"I'm just asking. But you probably ain't even from the South for real."
"Boy, I am from the South. I'm from Blackwell, thank you very much for your information!"
"Naw, I'm just playing with you shawty." Malik explained while laughing at her reaction.
"And what's your name?" Asked Keisha.
"Malik."
"What? You suppose to be some type of gangster or something?"
"Hell naw girl! Why you say that?"
"Because I see you got your black bandanna hanging out your back pocket."
"Oh! That's just because I like how it looks, that's all. So what, wearing a bandanna posed to make me a gangster?"
"No! But that's what all the so called 'gangsters' and 'gangbangers' wear."
"Naw shawty. I'm not a gangster or a gangbanger. The streets is already enough for me, but I can be a gangster if that's what you want."
"Nah, I'm good. I don't need no gangster."
Malik chilled with Keisha for the rest of that day. He met her aunt, who was having the

baby shower. He also became cool with some of her cousins.

Keisha's aunt decided to let all the kids stay over for the night. Malik and Keisha stayed up all night talking and playing.

After being awaken by the feeling of something wet in his ear, Malik realized that Keisha was sticking her fingers in his ear while he slept.

"What you doing shawty?" asked Malik, wiping the wetness off his ear.

"It's a Wet Willie!" replied Keisha as everyone laughed at the prank.

Malik jumped out the bed. "Y'all think some funny? Come here, since you wanna play."

"Aww stop Malik, let me go!" screamed Keisha in between laughs.

"Aight. I'm gone let you go if, you let go of my neck first."

"No. Put me down first boy, before you drop me!"

"On the count of three, we both gone let go."

"Aight, and you better not drop me either."

"Aight. One, Two, Boom!"

Malik slammed Keisha on the bed as soon as she let loose his neck.

"Ahh, Ha, Ha, Hah!" were the sounds of everybody laughing.

Keisha sat up and looked at Malik in shock.

"Why you slam me like that?"

"You wouldn't have been playing while I was

sleep."
"It ain't even that funny, with y'all ugly ass!"
yelled Keisha feeling embarrassed.
"So you mad now huh?" asked Malik trying to
baby Keisha up.
"Yep. Now move out my way with your black
ass!" Keisha stormed downstairs still wearing
her bed clothes.

"Alright. Y'all get y'all asses down here, right
now!" yelled Keisha's aunt.
"Mane, she a snitch" mumbled Malik as they
left the room to go down stairs.
"What the fuck y'all doing up there?" asked
Keisha's aunt.
"Nothing but playing" replied the kids.
Malik and Keisha locked eyes with each other.
"You snitch!" Malik spoke clear enough for
Keisha to read his lips.
Keisha read Malik's lips and rolled her eyes at
him.
"I know y'all hungry, ain't it? spoke the aunt.
"Yeah we hungry!"
"Well, y'all need to hurry up and clean this
house up so, I can start cooking for y'all."
Malik helped Keisha's cousins clean up the
living room. While straightening up the
Nintindo'64. "POP!" Malik felt something hit
him on his head.
"Don't you ever call me a snitch again!" yelled
Keisha as she quickly ran up the stairs.
Malik rubbed his head and tried to act like the

hit didn't hurt, while looking to see if anyone else saw it.

Malik stayed around and spent most of the day with Keisha, until that evening when he left to go on Phulpt Street.
"Big Cee, what's up bra?"
"Malik! Boy, where the hell you been at all day?" asked Big Cee as he dapped up Malik.
"I been at my people's house. Why, what's up?"
"Nothing. I just wanted to make sure that my li'l nigga was alright."
"Yeah, I'm good. What's been going on out here?"
"Shit. It's been slow out here today for some reason."
"There goes my baby right there!" screamed a light brown skin lady coming up the street.
"Who is that, your girlfriend?" Malik asked Big Cee.
"Naw li'l nigga. That's anybody's bitch."
"Big Cee, hey boo! Where the fuck you been at?"
"Shid girl, you know I be chilling. Trying to duck the law."
"Yeah. It looks like your fat ass be trying to duck me too nigga!"
"Hell yeah. Cause every time you come around, I'm always a few dollars short on the stash."
"Don't even try to carry me like that nigga! You know I don't want something every time I see yo fat ass!"

Malik couldn't help himself from staring at the lady. She was caramel complexion, slim waist, but thick in all the right places. She stood about 5'7 to 5'8 inches tall and Malik couldn't take his eyes off of her perfectly round, fat ass.
"Damn! Where the hell you get this li'l boy from?"
"That's my li'l nigga. Why?"
"Well, you need to tell yo lil nigga, its rude to keep staring at my ass like that!"
"Shid. Maybe, the li'l nigga tryna fuck you!"
"Big Cee stop playing with me! That li'l ass boy wouldn't know what to do with all this." She said rubbing her hands down the curves of her body.
"Yeah I would!" spoke Malik with a sly grin on his face.
"Boy naw, yo li'l ass! What you think you could do with me?"
"Girl, I'll have you in the buck."
"Yeah, you heard what the li'l nigga said!" laughed Big Cee.
"Don't do that Big Cee."
"Shid, it ain't me. My li'l nigga said he tryna put yo ass in the buck."
"See, you play too damn much! You need to take your li'l nigga to get his hair cut, with his nappy head ass."
"Girl, I can pay for you to get your hair done, with yo baldhead ass!" spoke Malik as he pulled a knot of money out his pocket.
"Boy! Who the fuck do you think you're talking

too? Cee you better get his li'l grown ass!"
"Get him for what? You shouldn't have called the li'l nigga nappy" replied Big Cee still laughing at the two go at it. "Yeah li'l nigga, that's how you do it!" He spoke giving Malik some dap.
"Don't do that Big Cee."
"Don't do what?"
"Don't be encouraging that boy to disrespect grown people."
"The li'l nigga must got you in yo feelings now, huh?"
"Nah. I'm just saying he grown as ah bitch. Plus, the li'l nigga caught me off guard with that shit tho'. Li'l boy, where you get all that money from anyway?"
"Get out the li'l nigga's business! Go to the truck and get me something to drink."
"What you want to drink?"
"It doesn't matter. Anything but soda."
"I'm getting yo fat ass some water. Is that it?" Big Cee looked at Malik. "You want something bra?"
"Yeah. Get me $2 worth of penny candy and something to drink."
"And what do you want to drink?" asked the lady.
"It don't matter."
"Now, is that all? With y'all funny looking ass." Big Cee reached in his pocket and pulled out a twenty dollar bill. "Yea, that's it."
The lady snatched the money and started

walking off. "I hope you know I'm keeping the change, with yo cheap ass!"

"Bra, who is shawty?" asked Malik while watching the lady walk away.
"That's just Nicole's li'l ratchet ass. What you like that jaint li'l nigga?"
"Hell yeah! Shawty look good as ah bitch bra."
"Aight. I'm going to get her to let you fuck her."
"Mane, stop playing! She already said that I was too young."
"Nigga, these bitches out here is down for whatever! They talk a good game, but they'll fuck their own child if his money long enough. So, you better know what you're doing with that pussy."
"Shid. I know what to do with it" replied Malik excited.

Malik and Big Cee were so busy kicking it. They never managed to pay any attention to the blue Buick, parked a half a block away from them.

"There go Nicole right there" spoke Big Cee.
"Let me holla at her and get y'all a spot to chill in."
"Here. Get this shit before I give it away" spoke Nicole.
"Let me holla at you real quick" spoke Big Cee.
"Boy, what do you want now with your worrysome ass?"

Big Cee walked Nicole into an apartment across the street.

"I need you to do a favor for me" spoke Big Cee.

"And you tried to act like I was the one who always wanted something though" replied Nicole. "What's up, what you need?"

"I need you to let my li'l nigga fuck you."

"What! That little ass boy! Who the fuck you think I am Cee?" asked Nicole furiously.

"Look, the li'l nigga likes you and he wants to fuck. Just do this for me and I got you" spoke Big Cee smoothly.

"I don't even know whose child that is and his ass might run his mouth too damn much!"

"Shawty, don't even worry about all that shit. You just handle your business."

"Aight. And he better not be all scared and shit."

Big Cee walked back outside and called Malik from across the street. Nicole went into the backroom and waited.

"What's up bra?" asked Malik smiling hard.

"You ready?"

"Yeah, I'm ready" replied Malik while sticking his hand in his pants.

"Aight, go back there and do your thang. Don't be scared, just go for what you know."

"Nah, I ain't scared. I got this."

Malik walked to the backroom where Nicole

sat waiting.

"What do you want li'l boy?" asked Nicole as Malik closed the door behind himself.

"Shid. You know what I want" replied Malik pulling off his pants.

"AH, HA!" giggled Nicole. "Boy, your li'l ass is something else. Come get on the bed."

Malik walked towards the bed with his young manhood standing as erect as it possibly could. He sat down on the bed next to Nicole.

"Damn! I see somebody knows what they want" spoke Nicole as she took hold of Malik's li'l dick. "Well, it ain't that bad. I guess I can work with this." Nicole began to suck on Malik's dick.

"Oh, Damn!" whispered Malik as he laid back and lost himself to a feeling he'd never felt before.

Nicole, sucked on Malik's dick while rubbing on his balls at the same time.

Feeling excited and confident, Malik stopped her.

"What's wrong boo, you finish?"

"Nah, I'm tryna fuck."

"Boy, you better know what you're doing too!" spoke Nicole, taking off her clothes.

"Do you have a condom?" asked Malik as he watched in amazement as Nicole's body began to reveal itself outside her clothes. She got the body of a video vixen.

Nicole sat on top of Malik. "Nigga, yo lil ass don't need no condom" she spoke as she slid on top of his standing dick.

Malik's body shook from the warm, gushy feeling. They fucked for almost forty minutes. After Malik finished, what felt like busting a nut, he began putting back on his clothes.

"Boy, your li'l ass ain't grown, but you know a li'l something! Next time I'm gone teach you some thang" spoke Nicole smoking on a cigarette.

"Who ever said that it was going to be a next time?" asked Malik with a grin.

"Boy, please. If I want it, yo li'l ass gone give it to me!"

"Yeah I might, but I'm gone holla at you later. I got to go."

"Aight li'l boyfriend" spoke Nicole in a sexual tone.

Malik left that house feeling like he was walking on air. It was his first time fucking a grown bitch and it was amazing.

Malik walked back across the street.

"Damn li'l nigga! It took you long enough didn't it?" yelled Big Cee.

"Naw, I'm good" replied Malik smoothly.

"Yea, you walking like you're the shit now" laughed Big Cee. "Look at you."

"Yea, shawty aight bra!"

"I told you I had you."

"Yeah you did that."

"See, these bitches out here ain't faithful. These bitches are only loyal to them dollar signs. So, don't you ever let a bitch know your business or the shit you do. Trust no bitch! Remember that shit."

CHAPTER FOUR

"Aight, there the li'l nigga go right there. I wonder what the fuck he was doing in that house." Spoke the nigga in the passenger seat of the blue Buick.
"I don't know and it doesn't even matter. Let's just go holla at Big Cee and the li'l nigga while we still can" replied the driver.
The two dudes got out Buick and walked towards Big Cee and Malik. Big Cee and Malik didn't pay the two dudes any mind.

"What the fuck!" shouted Big Cee.
"Y'all know what it is. Give it to me or give it to God!" spoke the taller one of the two.
"This how y'all niggas tryna carry it?" asked Big Cee. "Y'all gone rob the li'l kid too?"
"Nigga shut the fuck up! Don't nobody give ah fuck about no damn kids. It comes with the game. Nigga, you know that" spoke the shorter guy.
Malik stood dead still and kept watching the two dudes who held him and Big Cee at gunpoint, while taking all their money. He was determined to never forget their faces.
"Charge this shit to the game homeboy!" yelled one of the robbers as they ran back to the Buick and drove away.

"Niggas wanna try yo boy now though!" spoke

Big Cee manically.

Malik walked behind Big Cee with rage and fear flowing through every inch of his body.

"Come around the hood" spoke Big Cee into his cellphone. "Nigga, fuck all that shit! Come around the hood right now and bring some grills. We're about to have a cookout" yelled Big Cee oblivious to everything else going on around him.

They went into the spot across the street.

"Mane, this shit crazy" spoke Malik rubbing his pockets for money that wasn't there.

"Don't worry about that shit lil nigga, I got you" spoke Big Cee.

Finally, Big Cee's right hand man, Wolf, walked in. He stood about 5'9 and weighed about 180 pounds in lean muscle. Black as midnight with a baldhead, and was well-known for putting in work.

"What the fuck going on bra! You good, I mean what's up?" asked Wolf.

"Hold up real quick" replied Big Cee. "Aye Nicole!"

"What you want now!" yelled Nicole coming from the backroom.

"Go to the candy man and tell him to send me a box of Dutches."

"Aight. What's up Wolf?"

"What's up shawty" replied Wolf as Nicole walked passed him and out the door.

"Them bitch ass niggas Tone and Black, caught me and li'l homie slipping" spoke Big Cee once

Nicole was gone.

"They jacked the li'l nigga too?" asked Wolf in disbelief.

"Yeah. Them niggas took all my bread too" spoke Malik.

"How much they take from you?" asked Big Cee.

"Almost a stack and they got the rest of my work too."

"Just go home, holla at me tomorrow, and I got you."

"Nah, fuck that! I'm tryna ride. Them niggas took my shit and put the iron in my face" spoke Malik with his anger growing by the second.

"I know that li'l nigga. So, go home, let me handle this and holla at me tomorrow."

"I know you gone handle it, but I want to put in my own work" replied Malik looking Big Cee in his eyes with every word.

Big Cee gave Malik a deadly face off. Neither of them broke their stare, until Big Cee said, "Okay li'l nigga, you got it."

"What the fuck you mean he got it?" asked Wolf. "I know you ain't about to let this li'l nigga ride with us!"

"Chill out. The li'l nigga good, I got him."

"Yeah, aight! If the li'l nigga get to knowing shit, that's your business to handle too."

"Did you bring them things like I said?"

"Yeah, I got 'em" replied Wolf as he pulled 2 handguns from his waistline. "The choppa's in

the car."
"Here. Take this" spoke Big Cee handing Malik a grey and black 9mm Taurus.
"You do know how to use it don't you?" asked Wolf.
Malik looked at the unique piece of steel admiring the power it gave him. "Yea I know how to use it. You just pull."
"Hold up li'l nigga!" yelled Wolf, interrupting Malik before he pulled the trigger. "It's off safety."
"Yo, Wolf, call your girl and tell her to report the rental stolen right now" spoke Big Cee.
"You sure you're ready for this shit li'l nigga?" spoke Big Cee. "It ain't no turning back once we're gone."
Malik looked at Big Cee with a blank expression on his face, as he placed the strap on his hip. "Yeah, I'm ready."
"She's doing it now" spoke Wolf as he hung up the phone.
"Word. Now, we need to find out where these niggas live at" spoke Big Cee.
"Shid, that nigga Tone stay with that li'l freak bitch around Church Hill on 32nd street" spoke Wolf.

"Nigga, next time yo fat ass need to walk your damn self." yelled Nicole coming into the house. "I look too damn good to be walking." She threw the box of Dutches on the table and headed back to the backroom.

"Call your girl back and see what's up" spoke
Big Cee.
"Everything's good" replied Wolf. "She's
waiting on the people now."
"Aight, let's be out. You ready li'l Nigga?" asked
Big Cee.
"Let's go" replied Malik as they stood and
headed for the door.

Wolf was driving an all-black Chevy Malibu,
with dark tints and silver trimming.
Malik rode in the backseat as they drove down
the dark streets listening to 'Young Jeezy's -
THUG MOTIVATION 101'.
As Jeezy rapped, "I remember nights, I didn't
remember nights, I damn near went crazy, I
had to get it right!" The rest of the passengers
stayed focus on what was about to be done.
Malik sung along with the song in his head,
trying to get his mind off of things.
As they turned onto 32nd street, the car began
to slow down.
"There's the car them niggas was driving right
there" Malik spoke to Wolf and Big Cee.
"Yeah, that's the crib right there" spoke Wolf.
"Circle the block" spoke Big Cee as he turned
the music off. "Hold up! Nigga, how do you
know the exact house tho'?"
"Shid! Bra, if you ever crept with that bitch
you'll remember her crib too!" replied Wolf as
him and Big Cee shared a laugh. "Shawty can
suck a golf ball through a slurpee straw."

Wolf circled the block slow enough to see and fast enough not to seem suspicious.
"Park on the side street" spoke Big Cee.
Wolf parked on the side of one 32nd street.
"Wolf, you go and knock on the door since you know the bitch. When she opens the door, we go in and handle our business. Remember, we don't need no witnesses" spoke Big Cee.
They all got out the car and walked down 32nd street.

Without any street lights, 32nd street was nearly pitch black. Malik walked behind the others carefully observing his surroundings.
Wolf walked on the porch, peeped through the living room window, and waved Big Cee and Malik to join him.
Big Cee and Malik stood up against the wall beside the door.
Wolf began knocking on the door. "KNOCK! KNOCK! KNOCK!.. KNOCK! KNOCK! KNOCK!"
"Who is it?" yelled a female voice from behind the door.
"It's me!" answered Wolf.
As the woman unlocked the door, Malik stood behind Big Cee with his gun in hand and a rush of adrenaline.
When the door came open. Wolf wrapped his hand around the lady's mouth and held his .45 Smith & Wesson at his lips, signaling for her to keep quiet. Big Cee walked in behind Wolf, aiming his AK-47. Malik entered behind Big

Cee and closed the door behind him.
Malik noticed that the lady was only wearing a pair of boy shorts and a tank top.
"Bitch, you better not say shit and take us where them niggas at" whispered Wolf.
The lady began to walk up the steps, trembling with fear as Wolf had his hand gripped to her ponytail and the barrel of his gun kissing the back of her head.

The smell of weed smoke became stronger with every step they took as they reached the top of the stairs. The lady opened a door on the right side of the wall.
"Oh shit!" someone yelled as Wolf threw the girl to the floor and held everyone else at gunpoint.
"Nigga, I wish you would move" spoke Big Cee as he stepped in the room and took aim at the bodies sitting on the bed. "So, this what y'all go and do with my money?"
"Come on bra!"
"WHACK!" Wolf hit the taller guy in the head with his gun. "Nigga ain't nobody tell you to speak."
"Y'all must've thought y'all was good, huh? Up here chilling and getting high with the bitches. But y'all had to know better than that" spoke Big Cee. "Lil nigga, what should we do to these niggas?"
Malik never took his eyes off of the dude that held him at gun point and took his money.

"Dude right here said that he didn't like kids" spoke Malik nodding at dude. "POW! POW! POW! POW! POW!" was all you heard as Malik shot the dude he was staring at.

"CHOP! CHOP! CHOP! CHOP! BLOK! BLOK! BLOK!" were the only sounds left in the room as Big Cee and Wolf sprayed bullets on every living thing left in the room.
Big Cee turned to Malik. "Shoot everybody in here."
"POW! POW! POW! POW! POW! POW!" Malik did it without hesitation. Before leaving, Malik looked at all the bodies stretched out in the room.
They ran out the backdoor and down an alley to the car. They drove back to Fairfield in pure silence.
"Give me y'all straps" spoke Big Cee as he placed the AK-47 in a blue Nike duffle bag. Wolf and Malik handed Big Cee their guns and watched him place them inside the bag and zipped it close.
"Get rid of the whip and holla at me tomorrow. I got the rest of this shit" spoke Big Cee while he dapped hands with Wolf before getting out the car.
"You good li'l homie?" asked Wolf with his hand out waiting on Malik to dap him up.
"Yea, I'm good bra. Fuck that shit" replied Malik as he dapped him up.
"When you get the car, pick up some dirt and

rub it all over your hands" spoke Wolf, knowing that dirt breaks down the gunpowder chemicals.
Wolf drove off as Big Cee and Malik walked back into the spot.

"Where in the hell y'all been? I've been looking for y'all!" yelled Nicole.
"We was chilling" replied Malik while walking to the bathroom.
"Yeah right, chilling my ass!"
"Girl shut up! You ain't nobody's wife" spoke Big Cee.
Malik closed the bathroom door and started washing the dirt off his hands. He splashed water on his face and looked at himself in the mirror. He held no feelings as he stared at himself and thought about what he'd just done. Before leaving the bathroom, he dropped to his knees and asked the Lord for forgiveness.

"This is Ann Kipfer of the CHANNEL 6 NEWS. We are coming to you live from the City's Church Hill area. Where four victims were found dead on the scene inside of their home, here on 32nd Street. The police tell us that each victim died of multiple gunshot wounds. There's been no information given on any suspects at this time. Detectives are calling this the worse homicide case since the late 80's. That is all the information we have at this time. Police are asking for anyone with any information that will help to call your local Crime Stoppers. We will keep you updated as more on this story develops. Again, I'm Ann Kipfer reporting live from your CHANNEL 6 NEWS @ 11."

"That's crazy! I wonder who the fuck did that shit. I bet you it was somebody close to them" spoke Nicole. "That's fucked up how you going to stay in a hotel and ain't even tell me!"
"What you talking about?" asked Malik. "I'm not going to stay in no damn hotel."
"Yes you is, because Big Cee already told me, with yo lying ass!"
Malik looked at Big Cee puzzled about what he'd just heard.
"What? I thought you might've wanted some company" spoke Big Cee shrugging his heavy shoulders.
"How you know, I ain't already have somebody going with me?" asked Malik going along with whatever Big Cee was trying to do.
"My bad. I didn't know that you already had somebody."
"Well, it's too late now. You done already told her loudmouth ass that she was going" replied Malik looking at Nicole.
"Nigga whatever! Don't nobody have to go with yo li'l ugly ass" spoke Nicole pushing Malik into the couch.
"Nah. I'm just playing with you, but if you put

your hands on me again" he replied smiling at Nicole.

"Boy, you know you jaint gone do shit" spoke Nicole rolling her neck.

"I see the li'l nigga got yo ass wide already" laughed Big Cee.

"Please! That lil boy can't handle me. I'm gone have him and all his li'l money in a minute." Malik looked at Nicole as if she was crazy. "Shawty, you tripping!"

"Aye who I'm is, rubber band man, wild as a Taliban!" was the sound of Big Cee's phone ringing.

"Aight boo, we're coming now" spoke Big Cee before hanging up the phone. "Go out there and talk with Tiffany, Nicole."

Nicole grabbed her purse off the couch. "Y'all need to hurry y'all asses up!" she yelled as she left out the door.

"Look, stay at the hotel with Nicole tonight and chill until tomorrow" spoke Big Cee.

"How am I going to pay for the hotel with no money?" replied Malik.

"I'm going to give you the money and something to smoke on, when we get to the car" replied Big Cee while picking up the duffle bag and heading out the door.

"There his fat ass go girl" spoke Nicole as Big Cee and Malik made their way to the car.

Tiffany was driving a candy apple red Lexus, and from the looks of it, it was brand new.

"Pop the trunk boo" spoke Big Cee. He placed the duffle bag in the trunk and reached in Tiffany's COACH handbag. He counted off ten bills and handed them to Malik.

Malik counted the ten hundreds. "Good luck bra" he spoke as he put the money in his pocket.

"What's up boo?" asked Big Cee before kissing Tiffany on the lips.

"Nothing. I've been missing you all day" replied Tiffany.

"Well now you got me for the best part of the night. Oh boo, that's my lil nigga Malik, Malik this my wife Tiffany."

"How you doing Tiffany?"

"I'm fine, thanks for asking."

They rode listening to Monica, while Malik looked out the window at the lights of passing cars.

"Stop by that CVS real quick" spoke Big Cee. Tiffany pulled into the parking lot of the CVS on Williamsburg Road. If judging NY by the traffic of CVS, you wouldn't have thought that it was already after midnight.

"Come on li'l bra" spoke Big Cee getting out the car.

Malik hopped out the car and walked into CVS behind Big Cee. "I'm thirsty as hell! I'm ready to go get something to drink bra. You want some?" asked Malik walking towards the aisle that read, 'COLD DRINKS'."

"Naw, I'm good bra."

"Hey sir, can I help you with anything?" asked the store clerk.

"Yea, I'm tryna buy one of those prepaid phones" replied Big Cee.

"Well, we have two different ones right here."

"Just hand me either one of them jaint, and can you activate it for me?"

"Sure, that's not a problem. Do you want to purchase any minutes right now as well?"

"Yeah, put $20 on there for me."

Malik walked up to the cash register drinking a strawberry soda and eating a bag of cool ranch Dorritos.

"What you need that phone for?" asked Malik with his mouth full.

"I don't need it; it's for you. I'm gone have Wolf pick y'all up tomorrow for me. When you get back home, just be a kid. Don't try to do any extra shit until things calm down."

"Okay sir, here you go. Everything's all set up for you. You just have to charge it up as soon as possible. Now, would that be all for you tonight?"

"Yea that's good. I appreciate it" spoke Big Cee as he paid for the phone.

Malik walked out the store behind Big Cee without even paying for his chips and soda.

Big Cee handed Malik the phone and charger.

"Since you got shawty with you, you might want to stay at the 'SUPER 8 HOTEL'. It's a weekday so, it should cost about $40."

"Damn! What took y'all so long?" asked

Tiffany.
"The motherfucker at the register kept talking our heads off about nothing." lied Big Cee.
"Drop them off at the 'SUPER 8' so we can go home."
"Here, just pay for one night and give me my change back" spoke Malik as he gave Nicole a hundred dollar bill.
"Aight! You ain't have to say it like that either" replied Nicole.

When they pulled up at the 'SUPER 8', right in the middle of '7-ELEVEN' and 'THE WAFFLE HOUSE' Big Cee handed Malik a bag of weed.
"I'll get up with you tomorrow."
"I got you bra. Make sure you take your time." Replied Malik as he gave Big Cee dap. "See you later Tiffany, and thanks for the ride."
"You welcome."
"Bye y'all!" yelled Nicole as she closed the car door.
"We need to get some Dutches from '7-ELEVEN' too" spoke Malik.
"I hope you know that you're buying me something" replied Nicole walking towards the '7-ELEVEN'.

They left the '7-ELEVEN' and Nicole paid for the hotel room. The room came equipped with two full size beds, TV, mini refrigerator, A/C and heater, and a full bathroom.

"Who you looking for boy?" asked Nicole watching Malik search through the room. Malik just looked at her and sat on the bed. "I'm about to get in the shower, so don't come in the bathroom!" screamed Nicole closing the bathroom door.

'Let me plug this ugly ass phone up. I wonder why Wolf gone pick us up. Fuck it, I guess I'll find out when that time comes. Let me go ahead and roll up. Damn! This shit looks good as ah bitch.' Malik thought to himself as he breaking up the weed Big Cee gave him. "COUGH! COUGH! COUGH!" 'Damn, this some good shit. Let's see what's on TV. Malik flicked through the channels and found nothing worth watching.

He lay back on the bed. He could see the hot steam coming from the bathroom, when Nicole walked out with a towel covering her body. "Slide over some so I can get under the covers" spoke Nicole walking towards the bed.

Malik slid over as he noticed Nicole's fully naked body slipping underneath the sheets and blanket.

"What the hell you doing watching the cooking channel boy?"

"I'm tryna learn how to cook too shawty" laughed Malik.

"Naw. Your ass just high as hell! Let me hit that blunt too."

"Here." Malik passed her the blunt and picked up his phone. Looking for a ringtone, he found

'Young Jeezy's - Then What' and brought it.
"Who is that calling you? It better not be one of them fast ass little girls."
Malik grinned at her. "Why you all in my business?"
"Cause I want to be!" replied Nicole. "Let me see that ugly ass phone anyway." Nicole snatched the phone from Malik. "Your mama probably still be going through your phone."
"Shid, I'm a grown ass man."
"Yea, that's what your mouth say li'l boy."
"Why do you keep calling me li'l boy? My name is Malik.
Nicole's phone started to ring and she silenced it quickly. "This is my number so, you better answer this phone when I call you 'Lil Malik" spoke Nicole sarcastically. "You need to take them clothes off and lay in the bed."
"Just shut up and roll up."
Nicole began rolling up another blunt as Malik took off all his clothes except, his socks and boxers.
"How old are you Malik, for real?"
"I'm about to be sixteen." Malik lied. "Why?"
"Cause you look like a li'l ass boy, but you act so damn grown."
They talked and smoked until Nicole slid up under Malik and wrapped her leg over his waist.
Malik felt his dick grow harder the closer Nicole slid her hand towards it. "Yeah, I thought you said, that you was going to teach

me some shit?"
Nicole began seductively kissing on Malik's neck. "I don't think you're ready for all that yet."

CHAPTER FIVE

They were awakened by the sound of Malik's phone ringing.
"Hello."
"What's up li'l homie, you woke yet? asked Wolf.
"Yeah. Yeah bra, I'm good" replied Malik stretching to get out of bed.
"Aight. I'm on my way, and I'm gone call you when I pull up. Word."
"Word." Malik hung up the phone and started putting on his clothes. "Aye wake up! Our ride is on the way to pick us up in a minute."
"Damn! What time is it?" asked Nicole running to the bathroom.
"It's 8:12."
Malik finished getting dressed and rolled up another blunt. Nicole came back out the bathroom just as Malik began to light up the blunt.
"You feel like rolling this jaint before we leave?" Asked Malik throwing the bag of weed and vanilla Dutch beside Nicole.
"Who's supposed to be picking us up?"
"Wolf on his way. He's gone call when he pull up."
"Well, I'm going home and your black ass better answer your phone when I call you. My number is already saved in your phone so, don't try to act like you ain't know it was me

calling you."
"I don't do all that. If I don't answer, I just
don't answer. Forget all that extra shit."
Nicole rolled her eyes. "I'm just letting you
know Malik. So it ain't no need for you to get
all smart with me."
"Hello! Aight, we coming now" spoke Malik
before hanging up the phone. "Come on, Wolf
outside."
They left out the hotel and spotted Wolf
driving a silver Cadillac Deville.
"What's up bra?" asked Malik as he sat in the
front seat.
"Hey Wolf" mumbled Nicole closing her door.
"What's up shawty. Where y'all going?" asked
Wolf looking at Malik.
"You can drop me off at home" spoke Nicole.
No one spoke a word as they drove listening to
Richmond's POWER 92.1 FM RADIO.

They finally pulled up at Glenwood Farms
apartment, where Nicole lived.
"Thanks for the ride Wolf" spoke Nicole. "Bye
Malik."
"Can I get some to drink?" asked Malik.
"Yeah, but you got to come get it yourself."
Malik got out the car and followed Nicole to
her apartment.
"Sorry, but you got to take your shoes off at
the door" spoke Nicole unlocking her door.
"This is aight" spoke Malik checking out her
crib while taking his shoes off.

Nicole broke a smile. "Yeah, don't try to get comfortable in my shit!"

The living room was decked out with a Burgundy living room set. Cherry wood center and end tables with the glass on top, and wall-to-wall carpeting. A big picture of Jesus hung on the center wall over the big couch. The entertainment set was made out of black glass, with pictures of Nicole and others. The box flat screen TV sat in the center of the entertainment set.
"You can go and you get you something out the refrigerator."
Malik walked in the kitchen and noticed that the table only had three chairs. 'She might got kids' he thought to himself. He opened the refrigerator. 'This bitch filled up in here.' The refrigerator was packed with food, drinks, and fruits. "Who you live with?"
"I live by my damn self! Why?"
"I'm just asking because you got all this food in here."
"That's because I love to cook my own shit."
Malik grabbed a bottle of water. "What about your kids?"
"Unfortunately; I don't have any yet. I'm not too pressed on having kids right now." Nicole walked towards Malik and pulled him in close to her by his T-shirt. "So far now, it's just me, myself, and you" she spoke seductively. "You gone answer that phone when I call you,

right?"
"Yea, I might."
"MUAH. You better." Nicole opened the door
for Malik to leave.
Malik slipped back on his shoes and left.

He got back in the car with Wolf.
"You tryna ride with me to the barbershop real
quick li'l nigga?"
"Yea. I do need my haircut now."
"Yes you do! plus, I need to talk to you about
last night, you know what I'm saying?" asked
Wolf looking at Malik out the corner of his eye.
"Yeah, but don't worry about that. I think
shawty feeling me already" replied Malik as he
took a sip of water.
"Nigga, I'm not talking about that bitch! I'm
talking about that shit that happened last
night."
"What the fuck supposed to have happened
last night bra?"
"Oh, so you don't know what happened last
night huh?"
"Nah, I don't know what happened last night. I
must've missed something. You tell me what
happened."
"Ain't shit happen last night, and make sure it
stay that way li'l nigga!" replied Wolf nodding
his head while looking at Malik with a smirk
on his face.
They pulled up in front of the barbershop on
25th street. Wolf had already made an

appointment ahead of time so, they didn't have to sit long. They were in and out in less than an hour.

"Check this out" spoke Wolf "I'm gone drop you off around the way. Just do you and be yourself."

"What's up with Big Cee? He good right?"

"Yea. He good, but he gone lay low for a minute."

Wolf dropped Malik off around Fairfield and drove off.

"Yeah. Did you talk to li'l bra?" spoke Big Cee from the other end of the phone.

"The li'l homie good with me" replied Wolf.

"He played dumb as ah bitch. I fucks with that li'l nigga, he's going to be a problem in these streets! I'm glad we don't have to do him in."

"I got a good feeling about the li'l nigga myself" spoke Big Cee. I'ma holla at you later bra. 'Word'."

"Word" replied Wolf hanging up the phone.

CHAPTER SIX

Malik became neck deep in the game, and was too young to realize how far that scar ran. He became stoned to feelings, very violent, and aggressive with no tolerance for bullshit.

He built a good relationship with Keisha. For some reason, he felt comfortable around her. Whenever they stayed at her aunt house, they would have fun and talk until the wee hours of the night. Nothing else really mattered when they were together. He felt like a child with Keisha, but unfortunately; the childhood that he never had, had already came to a total end.

"Malik!" yelled his aunt. "Come here before you walk back out that door."

'Lord, she's worse some. And I bet she don't even want nothing.' Malik spoke to himself.
"Yeah Mah?"
"What you out there doing boy?"
"Nothing. Just playing and stuff."
"You ain't out there being bad or nothing is it?"
"No" he replied. 'I knew she ain't want nothing.'
"Don't you want to do your Mama a favor?"
"Lord, what you want now? I don't feel like cooking" replied Malik as he laid stretched out on the bed.

"Don't you want to sell these for me real fast?"
asked his aunt showing him a bag of crack
already bagged up.
"Yea. I guess I can sell it for you."
"Don't tell nobody and make sure you be
careful."
"I already know. Don't worry, I'm always
careful" replied Malik as he left out the house.

Malik hopped on his bike and headed for
Phulpt Street. He hadn't been on Phulpt Street
in almost two weeks.
It was early in the afternoon and niggas was
posted up doing them, some niggas sat in their
cars and made sells. Malik rode up and spoke
to everybody. Everybody knew that Malik was
a humble person. He was quicker to joke and
laugh before he made conversation.
He stayed posted on Phulpt Street, hustling for
hours, even when nothing was going on. After
midnight, it was only a few people left on the
dark street, suddenly this brown caravan
pulled up.
"What's up Unk, you good?" asked Malik trying
to make the sell. "I got some hard for you."
"Hold on young blood" spoke the driver of the
van. "Let me pull over."
The passenger of the van hopped out and
came across the street. He looked rough, like
he'd just finished doing some construction
work.
"What's up Unk, what you need?"

"Look here baby boy, I got this brand new gun I'm trying to sell. It's nice too."
Malik looked the dude up and down, making sure he wasn't about to try something. "What kind is it and where it's at?"
"I got it right here; here look at it?"
"Hold on don't pull that shit out right here. Walk with me in the cut." Malik walked the dude in the cut between two apartments.
"Now, let me see that jaint Unk."
"Look, its brand new baby boy. Fresh out the box too." Dude pulled out a small all black .380 Kel-Tek.
"Yeah, this jaint official" spoke Malik inspecting the fairly compact weapon. "How much you want for it tho'?"
"It depends on what you're willing to give me."
"All I got is some hard right now. Unless, you tryna hold it for me till tomorrow."
"I'll take the work, but lookout for me now young blood."
"I can give you six $20's of some good" lied Malik; he only had $10 rocks for sell.
"Come on now young blood! It's brand new, fresh out the box. I know you can do better than that for me, I'm hurting young blood."
"I got to buy the bullets and everything tho' Unk. Know what, I'll give you seven of them. Unk you killing me mane."
"Aight. Give 'em here, I'll take that."
Malik handed him the work. "Here, take my number in case you're ever trying to sell some

more."
"I already got some more in the van that I'm tryna get rid of now, but damn young'un" spoke dude examining the coke. "Why they so small?"
"Come on now Unk, you know them jaint good. Plus, I'm ready to help you sell the rest of the jaints you got too."
"Aight, aight. Walk with me to the van and let me show you what I got."
"When they made it to the van, the dude slid open the side door. Inside was a variety of weapons. He had all types of military assault rifles, handguns, and shotguns.
"Hell yeah, Unk!" spoke Malik, eyes lit bright as Christmas lights. "Hold on, let me call my peoples real fast. I know he might buy all this shit" spoke Malik excitedly.
Malik pulled out his cellphone and made the call.
"Yeah, what's up my nigga?" spoke Big Cee answering the call.
"Ain't shit bra. It's a nigga out here with some car seats for sell. These jaint fresh too!" spoke Malik.
"What kind of jaints he got and how much do he want for em?"
Malik took another look at the guns. "He got all kinds of jaints. The big jaints with the chest and arm part. He got the jaints without the back on 'em, and he got the small jaints too."
Malik looked at the dude. "How much do you

want for all of them jaints?"

"Tell him to just work with me. I'm trying to hurry up and sell them by tomorrow."

Malik relayed the message to Big Cee. "Yea, he right here with me on the blade."

"Tell him to give me about 30 minutes and I'm gone buy all of 'em from him."

"He said, can you give him 30 minutes and he gone buy all of 'em from you?"

"Yea, but tell him to hurry up because I'm riding with somebody and they trying to go."

"He say you got to hurry up because his people tryna leave bra."

"Aight. I'm coming right now li'l bra. Just make sure that nigga don't go nowhere" spoke Big Cee before hanging up the phone.

"He on his way right now Unk. It shouldn't be long, he stay right around the corner."

20 minutes later Malik's phone began ringing. "Hello!"

"Tell him I'm coming around the corner right now."

"Aight, I see you. Here he go, right here Unk."

Big Cee pulled up and got out of the passenger side of the Lexus. "What's up li'l bra, where the straps at?"

"Go head and show him what you got Unk."

"Damn!" Spoke Big Cee as dude slid back the van door. "Oh, so y'all the mahfuckers who broke into that gun store on J.D. and took them people, shit! They got that shit all over the news right now." Big Cee laughed hard as he picked through the guns.

Dude looked at Big Cee like he'd just seen a ghost. "Naw, that won't us."

"Shid, I don't give ah fuck anyway. How much do you want for all this shit?"

"Well, you can see they brand new. They ain't been used so, for all of em." The dude thought for a second. "Just give me five thousand."

"I got three thousand for you right now, for all this shit." Big Cee pulled out knot of money.

Dude looked at the money real hard as Big Cee started to count it.

"That's good enough!" yelled the driver of the van.

"Yeah, I'll give them to you for three."

"Aye Malik, go tell Tiffany to pull up behind the van."

"What's up Tiffany?"

"Hey! Boy, what are you doing out here this time of the night?"

"I'm chilling" Big Cee said, "turn around and pull up behind the van."

Tiffany turned the Lexus around and parked behind the van. They loaded the arsenal of weapons into the trunk.

Big Cee got in the car to leave. "Good look for calling me too, li'l nigga! What you doing out here anyway?"

"You know me. I'm just chilling bra."

"Yea, I know you brought one of those straps for yourself too."

"Yeah. I got this li'l jaint right here." Malik

pulled out his new gun. "But I need some bullets."

"Ooh boo, that's cute! What his li'l ass doing with that shit?" asked Tiffany in shock.

"This a .380" spoke Big Cee aiming the gun at the floor of the car. "That li'l nigga a grown ass man! I'm gone call Nicole and tell her to buy you some bullets li'l bra." Big Cee handed Malik back his gun. "You know I'm going to be spending some time with the wifey so, I'm gone holla at you when I get back out here. Make sure you don't be on no hot shit with that strap either."

"Aight, I got you bra" spoke Malik dapping up Big Cee. "Bye Tiffany."

Big Cee and Tiffany drove off. Malik hopped on his bike and rode home.

Seeing that all the lights were off, Malik went around to the backdoor. They kept the backdoor unlocked for him when he stayed out late. Malik carefully walked into the house quietly trying not to wake anyone. He made it to the living room and grabbed the fake plant his aunt had for decorations.

Malik always hid his money inside the flowerpot underneath the fake plant. He took $70 from his stash to account for the work he'd gave up for the gun. He placed the rest of his money and his new gun in the bottom of the flowerpot, and placed the plant back in the same spot he'd gotten it from.

It was after two o'clock in the morning and Malik was on his bike headed back to Phulpt Street.
"Aye boy, come here."
Malik stopped as he heard the females voice coming from the dark cut. "What's up, what you need?" asked Malik after seeing who the voice belonged to.
The person was dressed like a man. Wearing a wife beater, some baggy shorts, and all white Air Force Ones. As the person walked closer, her breast confirmed that it was a female.
"Aye, what you doing out here this late? I sit on my porch and see you out here every night by yourself. So, what you doing?"
Malik gave her a confused look. "All I got is some hard."
The lady didn't dress or look like she get high, but her question wasn't clear enough for him to think otherwise.
"Let me see what you got."
Malik pulled out his last eight rocks. "This all I got left for right now."
"What these s'pose to be, five dollar pieces or some?"
"Naw, they ten dollars a piece."
"Where did you get this shit from?"
Malik was growing tired of all the questions.
"Look, I'm just tryna help my peoples. So what you gone do?"

The lady pulled out a stack of money. "Here, take this to your peoples and come back and holla at me." She gave Malik five twenty dollar bills. "I'm gone be back here on the porch."
"Aight. I'm coming right back" spoke Malik as he rode back to his house.
He sat on his back porch for a couple of minutes before getting back on his bike. 'Maybe she's tryna put a nigga on with some big shit. Or maybe she's just bored.' He thought to himself.
He rode his bike through the dark cut in between the apartments until, he finally seen the lady he was just talking to.

"You smoke?" she asked sitting on her back porch like she'd said.
Malik looked at her mysteriously. "Yea, I smoke weed, but that's it."
"All I smoke is weed too. Nigga, just because I brought that shit from you doesn't mean that I'm gone smoke that shit! I'm just tired of seeing yo young ass ride around on that bike all night by yourself."
Malik sat on the porch across from the lady.
"I'm good, everybody know me out here."
The lady threw Malik a vanilla Dutch. "Roll up then, since you good." She began breaking up the weed onto a dollar bill. "Don't ever smoke with somebody you don't know unless, you roll that shit yourself. Mahfuckers be smoking anything these days and won't even tell you.

What's your name and how old are you?" she spoke handing Malik the dollar bill full of weed.

Malik proceeded to roll up the blunt. "My name's Malik and I'm eleven, but I'll be twelve in a couple of months.

"You only eleven years old and you be out here by yourself late at night like this? Boy you should even be smoking, but you're going to do it anyway so, I rather you do it with me. I'm Roe-Roe and this my crib."

"How long you've been staying right here? One of my friends used to live right here, but they moved and I ain't never seen you out here before.

"I moved here a couple months ago, but I just started staying here."

They smoked and chilled until morning came. Malik had already begun to like Roe-Roe, it wasn't hard to tell that she was a good person.

CHAPTER SEVEN

Malik has been waiting for his start in middle school. He still had some money saved up for back to school shopping. Since he'd been robbed he's been staying away from Phulpt Street like Big Cee suggested and just chilled with Roe-Roe.

While sitting on Roe-Roe's back porch, Malik spotted his sister Jay coming up the street with a couple of her friends. He'd decided to try and creep up on them and make them scared. He stepped off the porch, crept behind the bushes and waited for Jay and her friends to walk pass. But, instead of them walking past the bushes, they stood right in front of them. "How are we going to get your mama to let you stay over our house tonight? She don't even know us girls" asked the black girl out the crew. She was ugly with the body of a grown woman and she wasn't a virgin. Malik only liked her because she let him fuck whenever he wanted to.
"All I got to do is keep begging her until she says yes" replied Jay. "Eventually; she's going to get tired of me asking and let me stay. Watch!"
'Oh yeah! I'm tryna stay over her house too then' Malik thought to himself still hiding in the bushes.

"Do she know about you and the dude you told us about?" asked the black girl's little sister.
"No! Nobody else knows but y'all. And y'all better not tell anybody else either."
'What fucking dude is they talking about?' thought Malik.
"Did it hurt your first time doing it?" asked the black girl. "I know mines did, but my first wasn't grown."
"Yeah it hurt, but then it didn't" replied Jay.
"Who the fuck you talking about you're fucking?" yelled Malik coming from behind the bushes.
"Oh my God! What you doing back there?" yelled the girls in shock.
"Jay, come on here. You're about to get a whooping! I'm telling mamah you out here fucking so, come on" spoke Malik.
"No I'm not!" yelled Jay. "You need to mind your own business. Don't nobody say nothing to you, when you be out here doing it to all these girls around here."
"Boy, leave her alone! You ain't her daddy" spoke the black girl.
"Mane, shut the hell up before I beat the shit out of both of y'all" spoke Malik furiously.
"You better not touch them!" spoke Jay. Mamah told you to never put your hands on a girl."
Malik started walking towards his house.
"Don't worry about it. I'm telling mah and you getting a beating."

"You a snitch!" spoke Jay as she took off running towards the house. "I'm gone tell her you trying to lie on me."

Malik chased Jay to their front door. "Mah, Jay needs a whooping! She's out there having sex" he spoke running into his aunt's room.

"No I'm not! He's lying" yelled Jay, running into the room behind Malik. "Don't nobody say nothing to him when he be out there doing it to all those girls."

"So what, I'm a boy and I can do what I want to do. You can't!"

"You can't do what you want to do, you ain't grown."

"Mah, whoop her butt!"

"No mah, he's lying on me!" screamed Jay.

"Mah, you need to whoop her! I bet if it was La-La, you'll whoop her" spoke Malik speaking to his aunt's favoritism for Jay because Malik and La-La weren't her real children.

His aunt gave him a hard stare. "You know what Malik. Since you're so damn grown, get the hell out of my house! I'm sick and tired of your ass anyway."

"How you gone get mad at me because she's out there fucking?"

"Malik, get the hell out my damn house now. And I mean what the fuck I said!" yelled his aunt standing from the bed. "Jay, go in your room and get the fuck out my face. Right now!"

"But Mah, he's lying on me!" cried Jay as she ran in the room.

Malik stormed out the house with a fuck the world attitude as he headed back to Roe-Roe's house.

"Aye, what's wrong with you?" asked Roe-Roe getting amped up by the look on Malik's face. "What happened?"
"Mane, my mamah just kicked me out the house because I told her that my sister out here fucking. I ain't even do nothing wrong."
"Don't worry about it, you can stay here. How old is your li'l sister?"
"She ain't nothing but eleven years old."
"What! She only eleven years old?" asked Roe-Roe in shock. "Who is it she supposed to be fucking?"
"I don't know. I just heard them say that the dude was older, but I don't even care no more. They can do whatever they want to do. I'm not getting in it anymore."

Malik began staying at Roe-Roe's house. Roe-Roe was very generous, what was hers was his; she kept creases in their clothes by sending them to the cleaners weekly. They were like 'Bonnie and Clyde'. Whenever you saw one you saw the other, both fresh as baby powder. If one of Roe-Roe's girlfriends brought her a gift, they had to buy Malik a gift too. If one of them wanted to take Roe-Roe on a date, they had to take Malik too. No matter what Roe-Roe did or where she went, she kept

Malik by her side and treated him as well as she treated herself.

They became so close that they even worshipped the ground each other walked on. Nobody could speak bad about Malik without Roe-Roe speaking up on Malik's behalf and vice versa. They would sit up all hours of the night and talk about various things involving life and in a short time span, they built a bond that was made to last, forever.

Roe-Roe took Malik school shopping. Malik used the money that he had saved up and Roe-Roe added to it. She took Malik to meet her mother and family, at least all the ones she liked. Malik was accepted as family too.

It's the weekend and Roe-Roe's mother was over. She'd just finished cooking a big breakfast. Roe-Roe and Malik sat at the table waiting to eat.

"KNOCK, KNOCK, KNOCK, KNOCK!" A knock came from the front door.

Roe-Roe got up to answer it. "Who is it?" she yelled before opening the door. "Yeah, what's up?" She asked looking at the stranger suspiciously.

"I came to get my li'l cousin Malik."

"You ain't come over here to get no motherfucking body!"

Hearing Roe-Roe yell, her mother walked to the door. "Why is you yelling?"

"This nigga talking about he coming to get

Malik, but Malik ain't going no fucking where.
I'm taking care of him my damn self!"
Malik walked out of the kitchen and was
surprised to see his cousin standing at the
door.
"Malik, come on li'l nigga. Your mamah said
come home."
"Naw, fuck that!" screamed Roe-Roe. "You ain't
got to go with this nigga."
"Girl, calm your ass down before somebody
call the police. And you know that's not your
child" spoke her mother. "Malik, go ahead and
see what your mamah wants and we'll see you
later."

The screams from Roe-Roe's anger rampage
could still be heard as they walked off.
Malik's cousin was his only role model and
father figure. Before he went off to join the US
Marine Corps, he was always there for Malik.
He kept him laced in the latest fashion, fresh
haircut every two weeks, and picked him up
every weekend.

He taught him to be the man of the house and
to always protect his family. He taught him
how to defend himself and never to be afraid
of anyone who bled the same as he did. If
Malik had a problem with someone, he made
him fight. No matter how many, how big, or
how strong the others were, he would never
break up the fights. If Malik lost a fight, he got

jumped by his older cousin. This taught him to handle his own business and never depend on someone else because people weren't always going to be around to help him. He also stressed the importance of education in Malik's head. They were cousins but lived like brothers.

"Hop in the car li'l nigga" spoke his cousin as he unlocked his car from the key chain. He was driving a black-on-black Honda Civic with limo tints. This was the first car he brought for himself. The car sounded like a racecar as he started it up. Then, as the car became fully alive, the sounds of B.G.'s - Heart of the Streets Album came blaring through the speakers as they drove off.

When they turned onto Mechanicsville Turnpike, his cousin turned off the music. "Nigga, what the fuck is wrong with you man?" "Ain't nothing wrong with me" replied Malik. "Then why the hell as soon as I come to pick you up, everybody's telling me that you're out here fucking up? Auntie told me that you be staying out late at night selling drugs! Mane, I know you're not out here hustling nigga, is you? And keep it real with me cuz. You already know that I'm gone find out anyway." 'Yea, I bet she didn't tell you that I was selling it for her.' Malik thought to himself. "Nah, I'm not hustling, but I did a li'l bit." Malik didn't really want to tell him the truth because he

knew that he'd get mad, but he had to.
"You know I should fuck you up right? What the fuck do you be thinking about? What if something would've happened to you, then what? You would've put me in a fucked up position because you know I'm not going to let shit happen to you! Man, you need to tighten up for real Malik. You feel me?"
"Yea, I got you bra" replied Malik feeling bad about the hurt he brought onto his cousin.
"I came to pick you up so we could hit the mall and shit, but we can't do that now because you're out here fucking up. If they let me come down next weekend, I'm coming to get you. But, you got to stop acting stupid li'l nigga." He spoke as he pulled up in front of Malik's house.
"I know you already know better so, I'm not going to keep talking about it. Whatever you got going on, get over it. I'm always here for you if you need me. I love you li'l cuz."
"I love you too" replied Malik dapping his cousin up before getting out the car.

Malik remained at home and tried to make things work.
"Malik, I need you to go with Jay and La-La to the state fair" spoke his aunt.
Malik sat down on the couch. "I ain't got no money and I need a haircut."
"Here" spoke his aunt handing him a twenty dollar bill and smoking a cigarette.
"I still need $10 for my haircut."

"Well, yo ass better use that twenty dollars I just gave you!"
"Then, how am I going to pay for the fair? That cost $20 by itself."
"Make it work got-damn-it! I'm not giving you nothing else."
"You don't ever want to give me nothing anyway! I don't even want to go."
His aunt threw her cigarette, ran towards Malik as he sat on the couch. She grabbed him by the neck, sat on top of him and started choking him.
Malik had the strength to push his much bigger aunt off of him. Raised to never raise a hand at his mamah, he just stood and walked out on the front porch.
Everyone outside turned their heads towards the sound of his aunt screaming and rambling on, while talking on the phone. Malik went back inside, lay on the couch and tried to calm down.
A few minutes later, his aunt's son walked in with one of his friends.
"What happened mah?"
"That motherfucker done put his damn hands on me! I'm tired of his ass!"
"Why didn't you call the police and let them come and get him?"
"Because, I keep on trying to give him chance after chance, but now I'm done. I don't give a damn what happens with his ass no more!"
"I'm calling the police so they can come get

him" spoke her son already on the phone with 911. As soon as he hung up the phone, he started hitting Malik as he lay on the couch. They fought until his friend broke it up.
Fueled by anger, Malik ran into the kitchen and grabbed the biggest knife he could get his hands on. Everybody started yelling, "Put that knife down!" as Malik went after his cousin.
"Y'all stop! The police outside" cried Jay. Seeing the look of fear on Jay's face as she cried caused Malik to stop and put down the knife.
His cousin's friend grabbed him. "It's okay. Just calm down, everything's alright." He whispered to Malik.
The police came and the fingers were pointed at Malik. The police said that they couldn't remove Malik from the home because he was a resident. Malik's aunt tried hard to express how much she wanted Malik gone, but the police still couldn't do anything. The only thing that they could do was allow her to press charges for assault, which she chose to do. Hearing that, Malik walked out the backdoor.

CHAPTER EIGHT

Malik went back to living with Roe-Roe. He started his first year of Junior High at Fairfield Middle School in the County of Henrico.
The County school setting was a lot different from City schools. It was more freedom and less harassment. There were no metal detectors, you didn't have to get searched by security every morning, every student was given an Apple laptop computer whether they could afford them or not, teachers engaged more with struggling students, just everything was better than City schools.
Malik gained a lot of attention being that he was new to the school and very different than the other guys, plus, he spent a lot of time flirting with the girls.

He learned that county girls were more attracted to guys who were really from the projects than they were to county guys acting like project guys.

"Shawty, you need to stop faking" spoke Malik to this girl as they walked to class with their arms wrapped around each other. "You know you ain't ready for me yet! You're probably still a virgin."
"Boy whatever! You wish you could handle this" replied the girl.

"Shid, we can always go to the bathroom then.
Since you supposed to be so trained" he
whispered into her ear.

"Aye, that's my girl, dude!" spoke the girl's
boyfriend.
Malik turned to look at the slim, brown skin
dude. "Aye, well that's between y'all bra! I ain't
got none to do with all that" he spoke as he
and the girl turned and continued to walk to
class.
"Man, I said that's my girl!" yelled the dude as
he grabbed Malik's shoulder.

Malik turned around and started landing
punches. Caught off guard, the boyfriend
couldn't do nothing but cuff his head in his
arms in attempt to block the rain of punches
Malik threw at him.
A couple of teachers ran over and tried to stop
the fight. Fueled with rage, Malik pushed one
of the teachers and continued to throw
punches at the boyfriend. It took the school's
security guards to come and slam Malik to the
ground, in order to break up the fight.

"So what's wrong with you? Why were you
and the other kid fighting? Then, you pushed
one of my teachers for trying to stop the fight.
Now, I got a young man in the nurse's office
because he might have a broken nose! As the
Principal of this school, I can't allow that to

happen to anyone's child while they are on these grounds" spoke the Principal. "So, what do you suggest that your punishment be?"
"I don't know" replied Malik. "He put his hands on me first, so I hit him back."
"Yes, you did, and you kept on hitting him too! Then, you pushed one of my teachers. Now, that boy is in the nurse's office with a possible broken nose! His mother is on her way here and she might want to file charges against you for hitting her child! Listen, I want you to go and talk to your counselor and y'all come up with a suggestion on what your consequences should be for your actions."

Malik left out the Principal's office and headed to the school counselor's office.
"Bra! What you get the fighting for?" asked Jay.
"Because, some clown saw me talking to his girl."
"Oh. Are you okay, how long they suspend you for?"
"Yeah I'm good! I got to go to the counselor's office now, to see how long they gone suspend me. It don't even matter for real."
"Aye, everybody kept running up to me talking about you punished that nigga! They say, he's fucked up too. I'm tryna find him so I can see how bad he looks" laughed Jay. "Everybody knows not to mess with my big brother now. And when are you gone start back staying at home?"

"Mane, I don't know because mamah be tripping. Plus, they about to suspend me so, you know she's really going to trip now."
"Ringgggggg! Ringggggg!" was the sound of the school bell.
"You better go ahead and get to class" spoke Malik.
"Aight bra, I'll see you later. I love you" replied Jay giving Malik a hug before heading to class.

Malik walked up to the counselor assistant's desk. "The Principal sent me here to talk with the counselor."
"Yes, she's in there waiting for you" spoke the assistant. "The first door on the left."
"Knock! Knock!"
"Yes, come in!" spoke the counselor.
Malik walked in the office and found a pretty, blonde white lady sitting behind a desk. If she was old in age, it really didn't show in her features. She could've easily passed as a high school student.
"Well, you must be Mr. Matthews" spoke the counselor. "Mr. Matthews, what's the problem, why are you coming to school getting into fights?"
"I don't come to school to get into fights!"
"Then, what happened, why were you fighting? I know you weren't fighting for no reason at all."
"I don't know!" replied Malik getting frustrated. "I was minding my own business,

dude came and put his hands on me first."
"And this child, just walked up to you and hit you for no reason at all?" asked the counselor shaking her head.
"I'm new to this school and I don't know nobody but my sister" lied Malik. "So, when he said something, I didn't pay him any mind and kept walking. The next thing I know, he's grabbing my shoulders. So, I hit him back."
She gave Malik a crooked look. "Well, it says here that you live with your aunt. How do you think she's going to feel about this? What might she say to you when you get home?"
"I know that she's going to be mad, but I don't stay with my aunt. So, I don't know what she's going to say."
"If you don't stay with your aunt, who do you live with?"
"I could stay with you for one night, if you let me."
"Seriously Malik, that's very inappropriate!"
'Naw, what's inappropriate is the things that I would do with you.' He thought to himself. "I stay wherever I want to stay."
"Why aren't you living with your aunt? Your aunt is your legal guardian, meaning she's the person who's legally responsible for your wellbeing." She spoke with a hint of concern. "So why aren't you staying with her?"
"I don't stay with her because I don't want to. And why is you worried about all that? That has nothing to do with anything!" replied

Malik frustratingly.
"Listen Malik" spoke the counselor as she
stood to close the door.
'Mane, she can't be old! not looking this good.
Why would she even want to be a counselor'
Malik thought to himself as he watched her
make her way back to her seat.
"Malik, I am here to help you! While you're in
this office you can talk to me about anything. I
will never go and repeat anything that we talk
about in here, to anyone."
Malik just sat there expressionless, as he
looked into her blue eyes for some sort of
proof on how genuine she was about what she
was saying.

"You can trust me! Everything that we talk
about in this office is strictly confidential. I
could lose my job if I repeat anything you tell
me to anyone else. Malik, I can make things a
lot easier for you while you're in school, but
you have to be willing to talk to me and let me
know what's going on with you" spoke the
counselor pleadingly.
Malik took her on her word and decided to
talk to her. He talked about the altercation
between him and his aunt, which was the
reason why he wasn't staying with her. He
never spoke about selling drugs or the poor
living conditions he sometimes lived in
because he didn't want to chance his aunt
getting into any kind of trouble. So, he instead,

he talked about all the problems that he was causing at home in the eyes of everyone else. After listening to what Malik had to say, the counselor asked him to sit in the waiting area outside of her office.

While sitting and pondering mixed thoughts. Malik thought that he was tripping when he saw his aunt walking into the counselor's office.
"What you done did now?" asked his aunt as she walked in and seen Malik sitting there as if he'd just lost his best friend.
"I got to fighting" replied Malik.
"How are you doing. Are you his aunt?" asked the counselor. "Can I talk with you in my office for a second?"

After talking with the counselor, Malik and his aunt left the school. Keisha's aunt was waiting for them in the parking lot to take them home.
"Why the fuck can't you just do what the hell you're supposed to do? Your ass is in school to learn, not fight!" yelled his aunt as they pulled away from the school.
"Mane, dude hit me first so I hit him back" spoke Malik interrupting his aunt.
"I don't give a fuck if he knocked all your damn teeth out your mouth! That still don't give you permission to put your fucking hands on other people's kids."
"So I'm supposed to just let anybody treat me

any kind of way?"
"You know what Malik? I don't give a fuck what you do anymore. I see now, you want to end up just like your mama! Now, I have to talk to social services because your ass don't know how to do right at school, but I'm telling you right now. I'm not getting into trouble or losing my shit for you. So, if they want to take yo ass, I'm gone tell them to go ahead and take you because I'm done. I don't know what else to do with you."

"Aight! Do what you got to do, because it don't even matter to me no more either."

"See, that's your motherfucking problem now. You just don't know what to say out your damn mouth! Aw shit! Look, these people already here. Thanks for the ride girl."
"Oh, you welcome baby. Just come to my house when you're finish so we can talk" replied Keisha's aunt.
"That's if they don't lock me up because I'm gone kill his li'l black ass."

As Malik and his aunt made their way on the porch, Social Services were getting out of their city issued car. Malik's aunt invited them inside.
"Malik, you can go ahead upstairs and stay in your room. And don't come out unless you need to use the bathroom" spoke his aunt as

they walked in the house.

After the Social Services people left, Malik went to leave.
"Look at you. I don't know where in the hell you think you're going, but you know you're not supposed to be outside during school hours" spoke his aunt.
"I know. That's why I'm going in somebody's house."
"Well, don't take your ass back up to that school because you're suspended for ten days. And don't forget that you have to be in court on December 1st at 9:45. You better hope that that boy's mama don't press any charges on you too."
"Yea I know" replied Malik, as his aunt reminded him of the charges he faced for their altercation.

"Hello. Yea, where you at?" asked Malik talking on his cellphone as he brought a bag of weed. "You tryna come pick me up? I'm around the projects. I'm gone meet you on 26th street, on the side with the houses." Malik hung up the phone and walked to his destination while rolling his blunt.

As he sat on someone's porch, he noticed a silver Chrysler 300 turn onto 25th street and beeped its horn.
"What's up with you shawty?" asked Malik

grimly as he got into the car.

"Damn nigga! I can't get a kiss on the cheek or nothing. All you can say is what's up. I don't know what yo problem is, but don't try to take it out on me!" spoke Nicole, irritated by Malik's attitude.

"My bad. It ain't even like that." Malik grabbed her chin and kissed her seductively on the lips.

"Um boy, now that's how you greet a bitch! And why the hell you ain't in school?"

"I got to fighting and suspended for ten days so, they sent me home early."

"What were you fighting for?"

"Li'l dude seen me talking to his girl. Damn! What you wanna be my mamah or some? Asking me all these questions."

"I should be your mama! I already told you about messing around with them li'l fast ass little girls. These li'l girls can't do nothing for you but cause drama. Now, look at you. All this bullshit for nothing. And I bet you ain't even get your li'l dick sucked by the girl, but you fighting over her tho'!" she spoke waving her hand as she spoke. "Mane, you need to start thinking like a grown ass man, since you want to act like one. A real man, wouldn't be fooling around with no little girls who ain't got shit. Especially; when they got a bitch like me, who's down to earth and independent. So, you can't be mad at nobody but your damn self for being stupid!"

Malik looked at her while shaking his head,

with a smirk on his face admiring her words. Nicole mushed him in the face. "I don't know why you're looking at me all stupid for. 'Cause you know what I'm saying is true!"
"They pulled up in front of Nicole's apartment at a little bit after 1 o'clock in the afternoon. "Don't forget to take your shoes off at the door" spoke Nicole.
Malik walked straight to the kitchen and looked inside of the refrigerator before he did anything.
"Damn, you ain't cook shit! Talking about you love to cook. Where the leftovers at then?"
"Nigga, I work all week and I eat the leftovers for my lunch. So, you need to shut the hell up!"
"What time you go to work?"
"I work from 4 - 11, and you better be here when I get off. You keep going M.I.A. on me, but not this time" spoke Nicole sitting on Malik's lap and rubbing his head.
"Yeah I'm gone be here shawty. I ain't got nowhere else to be."

CHAPTER NINE

Malik has been staying with Nicole for the past four days straight. He just got a call from his aunt telling him that it was very important for him to come home now. When he got there, Social Services and the Richmond City Police were there waiting for him. The police placed him in handcuffs and sat him in the backseat of the squad car.

Malik felt hopeless as he sat uncomfortably in the backseat of the police car. 'What is this?' he asked himself wondering what was about to happen to him.

Social Services pulled up in front of this home with an elderly black couple standing out front. The police parked behind Social Services. The officer let Malik out of the squad car and took the handcuffs off him. The Social Worker explained to Malik that this was a foster home, in which he would be staying. Malik felt uncomfortable about that and expressed himself to the Social Worker. In return, she told him that there was nothing that she could do about it, but for him to try it. Somehow, someone got in contact with Malik's mentor and he and his wife quickly came to support Malik. They were hurt when they found out that there was nothing that they could do to help Malik. They stayed there with him for almost two hours expressing how much they cared for him and that they were willing to do whatever they could to help him.

Malik spent all night tossing and turning, trying to get to sleep. It was already uncomfortable enough with having to stay with some complete strangers. And the cheap bunk bed, that felt as if you were sleeping on cardboard, made matters much worse.

The next morning, Malik was walking around outside on the front of the house thinking. The lady came out and asked if he was alright. After hearing that he was fine, she went back inside.
Malik continued to think to himself while walking in circles. The circles got bigger and bigger with each lap, until Malik built up enough nerve to just leave. He was not about to accept being forced to live with a family that he didn't know.

Malik crossed Mechanicsville Turnpike and headed up Cool Lane back towards Fairfield.
"Malik! Aye Malik! Boy, what you doing? How did you get around here, who you with?" yelled his aunt as they pulled into the grocery store parking lot.
"Mah, I told you that was him!" yelled Jay. "I know my brother."
"Who you out here with?" asked his oldest sister Michelle.

"Nobody. I'm about to go around Fairfield" replied Malik.

"What did you do, don't you supposed to be with Child Protective Service's?" asked his aunt.

"Yea, they took me to some old black people house around Whitcomb. They had two other kids there that they'd adopted, a brother and sister, but I ain't like it, so I left."

"Well mah, you can't even be mad at him for that because you ain't going to stay with no anybody either" spoke Michelle.

"Where y'all coming from?"

"You know Jay had to go to court this morning" replied his aunt.

"No I didn't! What she had to go to court for?"

"Well, you know Jay growing up fast with titties and her ass already bigger than mines" spoke Michelle. "So, one day, I was just fucking around with her, asking if she was having sex yet. And you already know that Jay and La-La tells me everything. Now, I was just playing, but Jay told me that she was already having sex. She didn't want to tell me, but I got her to tell me who she was doing it with. Come to find out, Mark (Michelle's ex-boyfriend) had been raping Jay." Malik looked at Jay angrily. "Mane, Malik, I was so mad and fucked up about that shit! So, I called Mark and talked to him like everything was cool. I told him that we need to talk. When he came, I called the police and they locked his trifling ass up. You

know the Fairfield boys said I shouldn't have called the police. They want to kill his ass!"
'I told y'all she was fucking, but y'all kicked me out the house' Malik thought to himself. "What they say in court?"
"Today was just to see if there was enough evidence for them to take Mark to trial" spoke his aunt. "They charged his ass with sag-u-tory or stat-u-tory rape. Shit, I don't know how to say that shit. But, we got to go back in four months."
Malik was upset and extremely hurt by what he just heard. He had something's to say but chose not to say them. They all just got in the car and drove home.

"Look Malik, when we get home. We gone call that Social Worker and talk to her" spoke his aunt. "Tell her that you ran away and came home because you don't feel comfortable staying with strangers. You go with her, do what them people says, and let me try to get back custody of you."
"Yeah Malik, you just do what you got to do for real mane. I don't care if I have to go to court to get custody of you myself. We gone get you back home, believe that!" spoke Michelle.
They pulled up to Michelle's house. Malik's aunt called the Social Worker, who told her to keep Malik there until she got there to pick him up.

"Bra, I'm scared. Mamah said that them white people came and took you" cried La-La. "She said that you're not going to live with us no more!"
"Come here La-La. Don't be scared, everything's gone be alright" spoke Malik hugging his little sister. "I was getting in too much trouble so now, I got to go do some programs, but I'm coming back home. So, don't you worry about nothing."

"But, you're my only brother and I don't want to lose you! Now, I'm gone be out here by myself. So, what, you got to stay in a place like Bow-Wow in the movie 'Like Mike'?"
"I don't know, but I need you to be strong because if I know that you're sad it's going to make me sad too."
"Aye Malik, what's up bra?" yelled a dude walking up the street.
"Aight, what's up with you" replied Malik.
La-La looked at Malik suspiciously. "You know that boy?"
"Yea, I know him a li'l bit. Why?"
"Because he called me and Jay some bitches and said that he was going to beat our ass the other day."
"Why he say that, what did y'all do to him?"
"He was trying to talk to Jay and we starts joking on him and his mamah. That's when he kept calling us bitches and chased us in the house."

"Why y'all ain't just bank him then?"
"Mane, I ran because Jay scary tail ran!"

"Aye yo, hold up let me holla at you real quick"
yelled Malik walking after the dude he knew
from school.
"What's up with you Malik?" Dude asked with
his hand out to dap Malik up.
"Shawty, what's up with you calling my li'l
sisters bitches and chasing them in the
house?"
"Oh! I ain't even know" pleaded dude before
his word got cut short from a punch in the face
by Malik.

"Mane, look at this li'l nigga" spoke Wolf as he
sat in the cut and pointed everybody's
attention towards Malik fighting.
The dude slammed Malik to the ground and
was now on top of him. Malik couldn't get up
so he pushed his finger inside of the dude's
eye and pushed him off of him.
"I can't see! Aight stop! I can't see!" yelled
dude as Malik continued to hit him.
"Y'all stop it right now Malik!" yelled his aunt
running across the street to break up the fight.
Wolf came out the cut and went to help Malik's
aunt break up the fight. "Hold up!" Wolf broke
up the fight and stood in between both boys.
"What's up, you still want to fight him?"
"Naw. I didn't even want to fight him in the
first place!" replied dude rubbing his eye's.

"What you still wanna fight?" Wolf asked
Malik. "Mane, come on. The li'l nigga ain't
tryna fight you no more!"
"Oh nah! He ain't about to go nowhere" spoke
his aunt.
Wolf looked at her with a strange look on his
face. "Who is you?"
"That's my son! So, who the hell are you?"
"Oh, I'm so sorry! I didn't even know that you
was his mama. I look at your son like a li'l
brother and I just want to talk to him real
quick. If that's alright with you?"
"Yea that fine, but you got to hurry up because
somebody's about to come pick him up" she
replied before walking back across the street.
"Check it, chill out li'l nigga. Its aight to rumble,
but you got your mama out here tryna break it
up. Come on mane, tighten up and stop
drawing unwanted attention to yourself. Here,
take this and stay out the way." Wolf reached
into his pocket and gave Malik a fifty dollar
bill. "I apologize again mah!" He yelled across
the street to Malik's aunt.
"Its alright as long as you keep his ass out of
trouble!" replied Malik's aunt.
As Malik made his way across the street, the
Social Worker was pulling up.
The Social Worker talked to the family and
Malik told everyone that he loved them before
he left.

The Social Worker drove Malik to an

Emergency Residential Placement Program located on Parham Road. They pulled up to the front door and the Social Worker parked the car.

"Malik, I know that we haven't had the chance of getting to know each other. And right now, you probably don't like me much, but for some reason there's something that I like about you" spoke the Social Worker. "Well, next week is my last day working as a Social Worker so I'll be handing your case over to another worker." Malik just sat there half way listening to what she was saying.

"Now listen, the State is obligated to pursue the best interest for you. So, you better take advantage of your opportunities while you can. Make sure that you receive everything that the state has to offer you. Even if you don't need it, get it anyway. Don't just sit back and let people make decisions for you. This is your life and you do have a say in it. So, speak up and express what you want to do. Having your family on your side puts you at a great advantage. The state would rather place you in a foster home or with a family member because it's cheaper than residential programs. So, if you really want to get back to your family, take advantage of the system and don't let the system take advantage of you."

They exited the car to enter the group home. The group home's manager invited them into his office. The manager and Social Worker talked and filled out paperwork. When they finished filling out all the paperwork, the Social Worker gave Malik a hug. "Now, you remember what I said and do what you need to do; you'll be okay" spoke the Social Worker before leaving.

The group home's manager took Malik into the day room and introduced him to the rest of the residents.
Later that night, the conversation Malik had with his li'l sister La-La played over and over again inside his head. It pained him knowing that his actions had prevented him from being there for the ones he loved most in his life.

CHAPTER TEN

Malik has been in the group home for nearly two years now. He's been participating in several therapy and anger management sessions in order for him to go back home. He didn't care much for the sessions, but he learned how anger could be seen as a sign of weakness. This caused him to develop the skill set to think before he acted.

While reading the Richmond-Times-Dispatch newspaper, Malik came across a picture of Big Cee on the front page. He felt the blood boiling underneath his skin as he read the big bold captions; "RICHMOND KINGPIN SENTENCED TO LIFE, PLUS 20 YEARS IN FEDERAL PRISON."

He wanted to call around Fairfield so bad, but the group home only allowed residents to call the numbers on their phone list, approved by their social worker.

'What the fuck is going on out there!' Malik spoke to himself. 'I got to use the phone tonight.'
At night the group home staff change shifts and different workers come in.

"Malik, what's up with you man?" asked the

young staff seeing that Malik was still up during the middle of the night.

"I'm chilling bra, you know how I do. What's up with you? Aye look, I need a favor real quick bra."

"What's up, what you need?"

"Look" spoke Malik as he got out of bed and went to get the newspaper off the dresser.

"This my peoples right here and I'm trying to see what's going on. You know during the day, management be tripping about that phone list. I need you to let mc make a phone call to my people so I can see what's going on."

"Let me finish my checks and make sure everybody else is asleep first" replied the staff member as he left the room still reading the newspaper.

Malik waited for the staff to come back.

"Aight Malik, come on. You got one phone call and make it as quick as possible."

"Hello, can I speak to Nicole?"

"This her. Who is this?" asked Nicole trying to recognize the number.

"This Malik, shawty. What's up with you?"

"You li'l motherfucker! Oh, so now you want to call ah bitch after all this time? What happened to you? We've been looking for your black ass!" spoke Nicole, fired up.

"Mane, I only got a couple of minutes to talk because I'm on somebody else's phone. What's up with Big Cee? I saw that shit in the newspaper this morning" spoke Malik interrupting Nicole's fiery rant.

"That shit fucked up mane! His own connect set him up. When Cee called to reup, his connect told him that he was about to go out of town for a while. So Big Cee got 20 keys from him just to hold him down until his connect got back. Big Cee got pulled and took the police on a high-speed chase. The whole time, his connect was a Federal Informant. They had audio and video of Big Cee buying drugs from him. They say, every time Big Cee came back he brought more than what he did before. They had been building their case against him for five years. The Feds told Big Cee to give up Wolf and a few other good names, and they would work it out for him to be back on the streets within 10 years or less. But, you know, Big Cee ain't no snitch ass nigga. Instead of going to trial, he took the plea for Life plus 20 years" explained Nicole in between tears.

"Damn! So, what's up with Wolf?"
"I don't know. Ain't nobody heard from him. When he heard that Big Cee got locked up, he dipped and has been missing in action ever since."
"That shit wicked! I've been thinking about that shit since I read about it."
"Yeah, I know. What's up with you? Why ain't nobody heard from you in years? Big Cee be asking about you all the time too!"

"It's a long story, but I'm coming around Fairfield this weekend and I'll tell you about it when I get out there. If you talk to Big Cee before then tell him I said, to keep his head up. I got to hang up now shawty. You better answer my call when I get round there this weekend too!" spoke Malik, trying to get his grown man on.
"Naw nigga! You better call me this weekend. I swear, if I don't see you this weekend you better not even call me no fucking more, for real Malik!"
"Aight shawty, I got you." replied Malik before hanging up the phone.

"Is everything alright Malik?" asked the staff member.
"Yeah. Things just a li'l bit crazy out there, that's all. Good look for letting me call too."
"You know I don't mind doing what I can for y'all. So, what, this guy your cousin or something?" asked the staff pointing at the newspaper picture of Big Cee.
"Naw. He's more like a brother to me. He a good dude too."
"Well, I'm sorry that this happened to him. If you ever want to talk just let me know. I'm here for you."
"I already know. I'm about to go in here and go to sleep. Thanks again" spoke Malik as he shook the staff hand.

"Hello. Where you at?" asked Malik.
"Who is this?" asked Nicole.
"This Malik! What, you've forgot my voice that fast?"
"Nah. You just sound different plus, you keep calling me from different numbers. I'm on my way to the bank to cash my check. Why, where you at?"
"I just got around Fairfield."
"Stay right there! I'm coming to pick you up."
"How long is it going to take you to get back around here?"
"Oh, it ain't gone take me nothing but ten minutes at the most. Stay right where you at!"
"I'm on 23rd street across from Big Cee's grandma house."
"Okay, stay right there I'm coming now!"
"Aight" replied Malik as he hung up the phone and erased Nicole's number from the call log.

"Hey Malik!" spoke Keisha walking onto the porch with Malik.
"What's up Keisha?"
"Nothing. When did you get around here? They said, you was living in a group home. What, you back home now?"
"Naw. The group home gave me a pass to stay at home for the weekend. I got to go back on Sunday."
"Do you like living in a group home? I mean, how is it?" asked Keisha curiously.
"Its whack for real. All we do is programs,

counseling and a lot of extra stuff. Shawty, I can't wait to come home!"
"Do they let y'all use the phone?"
"Yeah. We got a phone list of who we can call tho'."
"Would they let you call me, so we could talk?"
"I got to ask them first. Aye, I'll be back later." Spoke Malik as he noticed Nicole's car pulling up.

"Boy, look at you getting big!" spoke Nicole as Malik hopped into the passenger seat.
"Yea, what's up with you?" asked Malik as Nicole kissed him before she drove off.
"I have to cash my check and make a couple of stops to pay my bills. I hope you ain't got nothing better to do."
"Nah, I'm rocking with you today."
"Aight! Now, what's going on with you, why it took so long for ah bitch to hear from you?"
"Well..."
"Hum, here go the bullshit! Come on with the lies" spoke Nicole shaking her head.
"Man look! I got to...." Malik explained to her everything that was going on with him.

"Well I have my own place, car, and a good job" spoke Nicole after hearing what Malik had to say. "I can go to court and get custody of you myself. Then, you won't even have to worry about all that bullshit."
"I thought about that too, but it'll be crazy. So,

we just need to deal with it for now. I should be back home in 3 weeks after I go to court."
"Oh yeah! I talked to Cee and he told me to tell you to stay out the way and he gone write you."
Malik saw the group home as he was staring out the window. "Aye, that's the group home I'm in right there."
"That shit is big as hell! I work around the corner so, I drive pass here every day."

Malik rode with Nicole until she'd finished paying her bills. He got her to drop him back off around Fairfield on her way home. Nicole tried to give him some money, but he refused to take it.
"I'm gone try to come back next weekend. Make sure you answer the phone when I call" spoke Malik.
"Okay. You do what you got to do and don't be getting into no trouble, so you can hurry up and come home" spoke Nicole before giving Malik a kiss and driving off.

CHAPTER ELEVEN

"Malik, where you been at? We've been looking for you!" screamed Jay excited to see Malik walk in the house. "Come on, La-La and everybody else is a couple doors down."
Malik and Jay walked a couple doors down to Keisha's aunt house.
"Hey bra! I miss you so much. I couldn't wait to see you" spoke La-La while hugging Malik.
"I missed you too!"
"Boy where the hell you been?" yelled Malik's aunt and oldest sister.
"I was around Cool Lane chilling." Malik lied because he didn't want anyone to know about him and Nicole.
"You need to tell somebody next time. You know you're not supposed to be out of my supervision. And you're not going to get me in trouble if them people decide to pop up and I don't know where you at" spoke his aunt.
"Aight" replied Malik.
"Malik, this my cousin Tanika" spoke Keisha, interrupting without excusing herself.
"What's up Tanika?" spoke Malik as they walked up the stairs.
"Hey. It's about time I met you because Keisha talks about you all the time" replied Tanika.
"Let me tell you. She calls me every day and all she wants to talk about is you. Boy, she's obsessed with you."

"Oh yeah?" asked Malik as if he wasn't glad to hear that.

"Nun unh! Don't do that Tanika. You know I don't even be like that" spoke Keisha.

"Keisha girl stop lying, yes you do! Malik, I'm telling you, all I hear is 'Malik this and Malik that'. She even be trying to figure out what she's going to wear when she see's you" spoke Tanika.

Keisha kept on trying to deny the truth, but it was already written all over her face from how hard she was blushing. She still tried to convince Malik not to believe Tanika because she was over exaggerating.

"Don't worry about it" spoke Malik. "I believe you Tanika. Keisha know she be thinking about me."

"Yes! Thank you Malik. She knows she do too, but now that you're right here she's tryna act all scared."

Keisha couldn't do nothing but cover her hands over her face. "Oh my God, that's so embarrassing!" Keisha spoke with a blush that displayed her pretty smile.

"Nah, it's not embarrassing. I think about me all the time too" spoke Malik jokingly.

"Yeah! So, you got jokes now?" asked Keisha playfully pushing Malik. "Who was that lady, that was kissing all on you, in that car?"

Malik told her that it was just a friend of his. Keisha thought the lady was someone's mother and wanted to know if Malik was sexing her.

"What you worried about all that for? I don't ask you about who you sexing."

"Boy calm down! I was just asking plus, you ain't got to ask who I'm sexing because I'm still a virgin."

The only thing that registered in Malik's mind was hearing her say that she was still a virgin.

"Mane, stop lying! You know you ain't no virgin."

"Yes she is and me too!" blurted Tanika.

"What! So y'all never had sex before?"

Keisha explained to him that she was scared because she thinks that it will hurt. Malik replied with his experience from having broken a couple of girl's virginity.

Keisha crept downstairs after everyone else went to sleep.

Malik woke up to Keisha kisses as she lay on top of him. Although a little shocked, Malik kissed her back.

"Malik, I want you to be the one who breaks my virginity" spoke Keisha staring deeply into Malik's eyes.

Malik met her gaze. 'Oh yeah, I'm about to burn this jaint up!' Malik thought to himself.

"Are you sure?" Malik asked soft spokenly.

"Yes. I'm sure, but I'm not so sure because I think you're going to try and treat me wrong after you get what you want."

"Shawty, you ain't got to think like that because that's not how I am. I want to do it. But, I don't want you to think that you have to do that for me to like you" spoke Malik, acting like he cared, but really just wanted to fuck.

"I want to do it, but I'm scared it's gone hurt too tho'!"

"It's not going to hurt. I'm gone make sure that I be gentle."

"Aight, come on" spoke Keisha after finally letting her guard down.

Wearing only a T-shirt and underwear, Keisha lay on the couch and allowed Malik to slowly lay on top of her.

Malik kissed and sucked on her neck as he lay between her legs. Keisha let out slight moans as Malik slid one of her legs out of her underwear. Malik grabbed a hold of himself and gently went to explore the inside of Keisha.

Keisha became scared as she felt Malik about to enter inside of her. She quickly pushed Malik in the bottom of his stomach and told him to stop. Malik tried to assure her that everything was going to be fine.

Malik got closer and closer to his goal, but being short on patience he grew irritated with Keisha for being so scared. So instead of entering inside of her, he just slid his dick up and down between the lips of her pussy.

Keisha moaned from the feeling while thinking that Malik has broken her virginity.

Malik continued this while kissing Keisha and looking at the clock. After five minutes had passed, Malik stopped and said that he was done.
"So that's it, that's all that happens and now I'm not a virgin no more?" asked Keisha shocked and thinking that she really just had sex.
"Yeah" lied Malik. "See, I told you that it wouldn't hurt like everyone said it would."
"Why did you stop? What you came?
"Nah, I don't even think I can cum yet, but it felt like it."
Keisha held Malik's dick and started caressing it. "Then, why is this still so hard?"
"I don't know, but it'll be aight."

CHAPTER TWELVE

All day, Keisha has been bragging and acting like she was the shit because she was no longer a virgin and handled the pain. But, little did she know. Malik had lied to her to get her to think that it didn't hurt, so he could get what he wanted.

"Malik!" spoke Keisha. "My aunt, your sister, and everybody else is going out to the club tonight. They gone leave the house to us and I want you to come over when they leave."
'Oh yea. Here we go, I got your ass tonight!' Malik thought to himself. "Yea, I'm coming over there. What time they leaving?" Malik asked smoothly not trying to seem anxious. "They gone be leaving in about an hour, they're getting dressed now. But look tho', and don't get mad either. Do you know Mack and Bo-Bo from around here?" Malik looked at her suspiciously. "Yeah, I know them niggas. But, why you ask me that?" Malik asked defensively. "Mane, don't get mad! But, Tanika talk to Mack, and Jay talk to Bo-Bo. They're trying to get them to come over and chill with them." Keisha noticed a slight frown forming on Malik's face. "Don't even start thinking nothing crazy because they just be talking and that's all!" spoke Keisha thinking that Malik was mad about his li'l sister chilling

with boys.
Malik smirked at the thought but quickly reminded himself, that he wasn't going to get involved with anything that his sisters did, after he'd gotten kicked out the house last time. "I got you. I'm about to go get them now." "Okay. When they leave, y'all come in through the backdoor."

Weekends around Fairfield were well entertaining. There was always something going on from: cookouts, house parties, block parties, and gambling parties. Tonight, there was a house party going on and Malik knew Mack and Bo-Bo would be there.
Malik entered the party as 'Gucci Mane - Bitch I Might Be' boomed through the speakers. He walked through the crowded living room looking for Mack and Bo-Bo. Finally, he saw Mack pinned to the wall by a girl twerking on him.
"Yo Mack, what's up with you bra?" spoke Malik dapping up Mack.
"What's up with you?" Mack replied with a smile and smacked the girl on her ass as she walked away.
"Li'l shawty Tanika people's going out to the club tonight and they want me, you, and Bo-Bo to slide over there when they leave."
"Hell yeah! Let me find that nigga Bo-Bo."
They found Bo-Bo and left the party. Malik knew Mack and Bo-Bo from school and around

the neighborhood. He was already cool with Mack and, Mack and Bo-Bo are childhood best friends.

"Aye, you smoke?" asked Mack as they sat at the bus stop, waiting for the women to leave.
"Yea. It's been a minute, but I still smoke" replied Malik.
"Why we don't be seeing you out here no more."
"I got put in a group home for some bullshit."
"Ah group home! What, on some Annie shit?" asked Bo-Bo passing the blunt.
"Yeah, some like that."
"Damn bra, I hope you ain't in there getting bullied by them white boys" joked Bo-Bo.
"Nigga hell naw! I'm the one who'll be doing the bullying."
They sat there and continued joking around until, they saw the ladies leaving the house.

"Malik, make sure you don't go nowhere and leave my door unlocked. And you better not have nobody in my house while I'm gone!" yelled his sister Michelle before getting into the car.
"I know. I ain't gone be nowhere but on the porch" replied Malik watching them get into the car and pulling off.
"Come on, let's go!" spoke Bo-Bo excitedly.
"Hold on nigga. Wait a second so it don't look obvious" spoke Mack smoking the last of the

blunt.

"I'm gone meet y'all around back" spoke Malik dapping them up to confuse any on-lookers.

Malik walked in the front door of Michelle's house, locked it behind himself, and left right back out the backdoor. As he was closing the door, Mack and Bo-Bo were already walking through the cut. They all walked and knocked on Keisha's aunt backdoor. Less than ten seconds later, the door was unlocked and opened by Tanika.

"What took y'all so long?" asked Tanika standing in her boy shorts and a tank top.

"I had to lock the door first" replied Malik as he opened the refrigerator and grabbed the jug of Kool-Aid.

"Damn right bra! Where the cups at?" asked Bo-Bo.

"Look at y'all li'l thirsty black asses! Make sure y'all wash them cups out too" spoke Tanika.

"Shid, what y'all got to eat in this mahfucker?" asked Mack as he went to open the refrigerator.

"Boy naw! Get yo fat hungry ass up out of there! Y'all done got high and now y'all got the munchies. Come on" yelled Tanika, pushing all three of them into the living room.

When they entered the living room, there sat Keisha and Jay on separate couches. The room was lit by the TV, but the only sounds came from music playing through the stereo system.

Malik, Mack, and Tanika all sat on the same couch with Keisha. Bo-Bo went and sat on the shorter couch with Jay.
"What's up, you trying to go upstairs so we can be by ourselves?" Malik asked like a man on a mission.
"Come on" replied Keisha.
"Look at they sneaky ass tryna creep off already" spoke Tanika as Malik and Keisha made their way upstairs.

Mack and Bo-Bo looked on in shock. They've been spending time with the girls for months now. Usually; they would bring an extra nigga along with them to keep Keisha company, but this was the first time they saw her actually engaged. It was utterly shocking seeing her walk Malik upstairs.

Keisha led Malik into her aunt's room. Malik noticed a portable Radio/CD Player sitting beside the dresser. As Keisha went and sat on the bed, Malik opened the CD player. Inside was a CD that read, "SLOW JAMZ MIX". Malik closed the CD player and pressed play. The sounds of "Joe - All The Things Your Man Won't Do" came through the speakers. Malik walked over to Keisha sitting on the King Size bed, wearing a white T-shirt, and stepped between her legs. He placed his hand underneath her chin and gently stared into her warm eyes. He leaned in and softly kissed her lips. Keisha passionately kissed him back. Seeing that she has began to loosen up, Malik decided that it was time to take control.

"Go ahead and lay on the bed" ordered Malik. While Keisha slid onto the bed, Malik took off his clothes and slid in bed on top of Keisha. He resumed kissing her and made his way to her neck.

"Mmm, mm." Keisha moaned. Malik helped her out of her shirt revealing her breast. He took one of her tits and guided her nipple to his mouth. Slight moans of anticipation escaped her lips as he faintly bit into her breast while simultaneously sucking on her nipple. He slowly made his way down to her thighs with trails of soft kisses. Keisha shivered with every touch. He looked into her eyes enjoying the way she squirmed beneath him as he prayed over her pussy. He slid his hands up her thighs and cuffed her ass as his tongue danced upon her clit. He flicked his tongue as fast as he could across her clit while breaking the surface of her pussy with his fingers.

Keisha shuddered from the feel of Malik's tongue washing her most delicate spot. She grabbed a hold of the back of his head and pressed it firmly against her pussy, with her body arched back as burning sensation shot through her flesh. "Ooooh!" she cries out of passion as her body buckles uncontrollably. Malik slid from between her legs and licked his lips, enjoying the last taste of her gracious fruit. He slowly slid back on top of her and began kissing her neck while caressing her nipple.

"Mmm!" She moaned.

Malik looked into her innocent eyes as he took hold of his hard and throbbing dick, and guided it towards the gates of her garden. He kisses her, vigorously letting his tongue roam the inside of her mouth as he slowly pushes his dick through her gates. He pushes gently, allowing his dick to explore fertile ground.

"Ooooh!" She squeals while digging her nails deep into his back as her body grips his manhood, like a glove, with every push.

He travels deep into her garden. Steadying himself, he launched one slow, but powerful thrust.

Immediately, Keisha started to shake uncontrollably with unexplainable passion. "Awe!" she gasps, digging her fingers deeper into his back as they both felt her insides "Pop". "Oh my God!" she squeaks, trying to brace herself as sparks of passion ignites a fire throughout her entire body.

Malik held on to her waist as she kept a deadly grip on his back. He slowly penetrates in and out of her pussy. She let out faint moans as the fire inside sets off fireworks, causing her to see stars.

At that moment, the lights flicked on. Caught in mid stroke nakedly uncovered, Malik turns around in fear.

"Ooh, Y'all so nasty!" spoke Tanika with Mack, Bo-Bo, and Jay standing behind her.
"Get yo nosey ass out!" yelled Keisha.
"Um, nice butt, boy" spoke Tanika as they giggled their way back out the room.
Malik and Keisha continued on with their session. Nearly an hour and a half later they were finished, both satisfied but hungry for more.

"Boy, that was a lot different than what we did last night" spoke Keisha while lying on Malik's chest. "What, your dick grew bigger over night or you took some pills or something? It hurt, but it felt good."
"Nah. Its just because we didn't really do nothing last night. I faked like we did because you was too scared."
"What!" Keisha jumped up. "So you mean to tell me, that you had me thinking that I was the shit all day and you didn't even do nothing?"
"Yeah." Malik replied calmly.
'Smack'! "That's fucked up. You's a liar mane, that's terrible" spoke Keisha feeling real stupid.
"Come on shawty, don't even do that. I didn't lie. You wanted it to happen so I got it done. You was so scared because you thought it was going to hurt so, I tricked you so you'd let your

guard down. I was just trying to make it easier, that's all. But look, it's almost time for your people to come back so, we better leave" spoke Malik as he started to get dress.
Keisha threw on her T-shirt and followed Malik downstairs.

"Y'all ready to dip? Y'all know their people about to come back from the club" spoke Malik.
"Yea, let's be out" replied Bo-Bo.
They all left back out the backdoor. Before Malik made it out the door, Keisha hugged and passionately kissed him as if it would be her last time.
"You better not try and carry me mane" spoke Keisha with her arm wrapped around his neck.
"The only way I can carry you is if you carry yourself. As long as you respect yourself, I got you" replied Malik, referring to a lesson his godmother taught him.
He kissed her again and left.

"Aye Bra, you was burning that jaint up!" joked Mack.
"I tried to do a li'l some" Malik joked back.
"So how long you gone be around here."
"I have to go back to the group home in the morning. I'm gone try to come back out here next weekend tho'."
"Shid, when you come back around here, come and chill with us. And keep yo head up bra"

spoke Mack as he and Malik dapped up.
"Yeah, keep yo head up bra" spoke Bo-Bo as he dapped up Malik.
"I'll holla at y'all" yelled Malik as he turned to walk in the house.

CHAPTER THIRTEEN

While back at the group home. Malik has been looking forward to his next home visit this weekend. And with only two weeks until his next court date, when Social Services would be recommending that he be sent back to live with his aunt, Malik couldn't have felt any happier.

Malik sat in his room, laid back in deep thought, listening to 'Akon's - Konvicted' album.
"Malik" spoke the staff. "They need you downstairs in the manager's office."
Malik stepped into his Adidas slippers and headed down to the manager's office, wearing nothing but basketball shorts and a wife beater. He tapped on the door before he entered and there sat the group home's manager sitting behind his desk, talking to a middle aged white woman.
"You wanted me?" asked Malik.
"Yes, Malik come in" replied the manager. "I want to introduce you to Ms. Lightford."
"Hi Malik. My name is Ms. Lightford and I'm your Guardian Ad Litem."
"How you doing?" replied Malik. "I thought that my Social Worker was my legal guardian."
"Yes he is. He is your legal guardian for placement and things like that for you, but I'm

your guardian for court matters, meaning, I tell the judge what I think is best and, nine times out of ten, what I say in court is what will happen" explained Ms. Lightford.

"Hold on. I thought that y'all was gone let me go back home after court?"

"Well, that's why I'm here. To tell you that that's not going to happen on this court date. When we go to court, I'm going to tell the judge that I don't think you should move back home yet. I think that it's best for you to continue placement in a structured program. So you can participate in therapy and get the help you need. Now, I know that this is not what you wanted to hear, but trust me Malik, this is what's best for you."

"How the fuck, you think you know what's best for me!" spoke Malik angrily. "You don't even know me, but you already know what's best for me. Then, you gone try and tell me to trust you! If I was to tell you the same thing that you just told me, would you trust me? No, you wouldn't. You'd probably tell me to kiss yo ass. Look shawty, I don't like none of this, but I ain't got no other choice now, do I? Mane, as long as I can keep going home on the weekends I'll do it" replied Malik trying to calm himself.

"Of course you can stay with your family on the weekends. Just as long as you're doing what you're supposed to do and it's approved by the group home."

"Aight. I'm going back to my room."
"Well, it was nice to finally meet you, even under these circumstances. I'm sorry that things aren't going how you would like them to."
"Yeah, I wish I could say the same" replied Malik as he shook her hand and left the office. Malik went back into his room, lay on the bed and listened to his music until he fell asleep.

On Friday, his aunt came to pick him up. They left the group home and headed to Fairfield. When they got home, Malik's sister was walking out the front door.
"Hey boo!" spoke Michelle excitedly. "Boy, I missed your li'l black ass" she spoke giving him a hug.
"I missed you too" replied Malik. "Let me see your phone real quick."
"Here. Who the hell you calling already."
"This girl I just met" Malik lied.
"Aye, you better not let Keisha find out because she's going to kill you if she do! Let me tell you, that girl has been asking about you all week too."
"She ain't gone find out" replied Malik walking towards the bus stop to call Nicole. "Yea, where you at? Aight come pick me up from out front of Fairfield Elementary School" He told Nicole before hanging up the phone. "Aye mah, I'm about to go around the street to my friend house."

"Okay, but make sure you bring your ass back and be careful!" yelled his aunt.

Malik spoke to everyone he knew as he walked down Phulpt Street to meet Nicole. Nicole was already parked out front the school when he got there. He hopped in the passenger seat. "What's up shawty?" he spoke as he closed the door.
"Yeah, your black ass better had called me."
"Do you ever stop talking shit?" he asked bcfore giving her a kiss.
"Hell naw! If I'm not talking shit, something's wrong. Here." Nicole reached into her purse and handed him an envelope. "This is for you."
Malik opened the envelope. Inside was a letter which read:

'Aye, what's happening with you li'l homie? You already know, Nicole told me about what's going on with you out there. You better be keeping your head up and not letting that shit get the best of you. "What doesn't kill a boy, only makes a stronger man."
Yeah, my time out there is over, but the game never stops. As a man, I had to take that plea and lay it down because snitching is never an option. I'm not going to talk you to death. I just want to let you know something:
"In life, there's consequences behind everything that you do whether it's good or bad. So, before you do anything, know what

the consequences will be behind it because you're the only one who has to deal with them, when that time comes."
You're my li'l nigga, so if you ever need anything, just holla at my wife or Nicole. I've already let them know, what's mine is yours. Just be smart.
I'm out for now. Li'l nigga, stay real and always keep your head up. Remember: "Real Niggaz Stand Tall, bitch niggas sit down!"
One Love,
Big Cee!

Malik finished reading the letter at the same time they pulled up in front of Nicole's house. Nicole put her car in park and they got out.
"Don't forget to take your shoes off" she spoke as they arrived at the front door.
They entered Nicole's house and Malik noticed that everything was exactly the same as the last he was here.
Nicole went into the kitchen and Malik watched how her ass bounced as she walked. Lustfully, he walked behind her.
"Do you want something to eat?" she asked bent over reaching inside of the refrigerator.

"Nah, I'm good" he replied grabbing her by the waist and grinding against her ass. Grinding from side to side, he could feel that she didn't have on any underwear underneath her pink Aeropostale sweatpants. This enticed him more.

"Nigga, you scared the shit out of me! I ain't." spoke Nicole as she turned around. But, her words were cut short by Malik kissing her. Instinctively, she became sexually aggressive. She sucked on his neck as she unbuckled his belt. While looking into his eyes, she slowly slid to her knee's and pulled his dick out his pants. With a firm grip, she begins massaging his dick as she kisses its head, while fondling his balls. A wicked smile flashes across her face as she feels his dick getting harder. She licks her lips and her tongue flicks across the head of his dick as her lips slowly closes around its length.

Malik grabbed a fist full of her hair from the back of her head and slowly started fucking her face.

Nicole forcefully grabbed him by his ass cheeks and rammed him into her face. She stroked his dick and started humming as she sucked and swallowed. This sent a feeling of vibration through his dick and up his spine. With Nicole still looking in his eyes, Malik just grinned back at her. He stood on his tippy toes as she caused him to shake with pleasure. Nicole ended by stroking his dick while sucking on the head, as she looked up at Malik, who had his head leaned back as if it was broken.

Nicole went upstairs to freshen up. As she did

that, Malik took out the letter that Big Cee wrote him and read it again.

After reading the letter, Malik sat and thought about the plan that he'd came up with after plotting all week.

"Why you ain't turn the TV on or something?" asked Nicole coming down the stairs.

"Shid, I ain't even feel like turning it on. Do you feel like taking me to the store?"

"Yeah. What you need from the store?"

"I need to get one of those prepaid phones."

"Why are you going to buy a phone? I thought you said, they won't let y'all have phone in the group home."

"We can't have phones, but I'm getting one anyway."

On the way to Walgreen's, Malik explained to Nicole the reason why he needed to buy the phone.

After leaving the store and buying a Motorola flip phone, they went back to Nicole's house. They talked and ate while Malik charged up his phone. At 9:45 PM, they got into Nicole's car and pulled off.

By ten o'clock, they were driving into the group home's compound, where Malik stayed. He pointed her in the direction of the gym. Nicole parked in front of the gym and Malik got out of the car.

Malik walked along the side to the back of the gym. He searched for a good hiding place.

Finally, his eyes landed on a bush beside the A/C unit. He hid the phone and its charger inside the bush and went back to the car. They left the group home and Nicole took Malik back home. When they pulled up, Malik spotted Mack and Bo-Bo sitting on Keisha's aunt porch.

"Remember, I'm not going to ask for any more home passes. So, make sure you be ready" spoke Malik.

"Oh, I'll be ready. You make sure you keep yo ass out of trouble" replied Nicole giving him a kiss goodbye and driving home

"What's up with y'all niggas?" asked Malik.

"Ain't shit. What's up with you?" replied Bo-Bo and Mack.

"Nothing. Hold on real quick, I'll be back" spoke Malik before walking in the house. After letting his aunt know that he was back and going to be out on the porch, he went back outside.

"What y'all niggas doing?" asked Malik dapping them both up.

"We was waiting for them to come back outside, but we about to go smoke a blunt now. You tryna blow?" spoke Bo-Bo.

"Yea, let's be out" replied Malik.

They all left the porch and walked to the playground at the bottom part of Fairfield projects. From where they sat, they could see the whole of Seldon Street and 25th Street.

"So what's going on with you bra?" Mack asked Malik.

"Ain't none for real. These mahfucking people tripping, talking about they not trying to let ah nigga come back home."

"What they mean, they not letting you come back home?" asked Bo-Bo.

"Mane, they talking about they want me to do all these therapy and anger management programs and shit, but fuck that! I'm about to buck on that shit bra."

"Hell yea! I'll buck on that shit too bra, if I was you" spoke Bo-Bo.

"Shid bra. We got a spot for you, if you do buck on that shit. Them people wild as ah bitch for that" spoke Mack.

They continued to smoke and talk as they watched everything that was going on around them.

CHAPTER FOURTEEN

Malik woke up and showered before going downstairs for breakfast. After breakfast, he went back to his room to get dress for court. He decided to wear a plain white T-shirt, black Rocawear denim jeans, and a pair of all white mid-top Nike Air Force Ones. He stayed in his room listening to Young Jeezy's - Thug Motivation 101 album as he waited for his social worker to come pick him up.

His social worker arrived a little bit after 9:30 AM. Malik's court hearing wasn't until quarter after ten. On the way to the courthouse, his social worker listened to some bullshit ass talk show on the radio and Malik just stared out the window into space as they made it to the courthouse.
Before being called to go in front of the judge, Malik sat in the waiting room talking with his aunt. She tried encouraging him that everything was going to be fine, even though things weren't going to go how they had hoped they would.

After court, Malik's social worker offered to take him out for lunch, but he insisted on going straight back to the group home.

Malik couldn't help himself from being angry

about what happened in court, even though he already knew what the outcome was going to be. He made sure he kept his composure and didn't show any signs of anger as he went along with his daily routine and went to bed on time.

He woke up at one o'clock in the morning and grabbed his cell phone out of the dresser. He packed his Nike book bag with only boxer shorts and hygiene items. He got dressed and waited for what felt like an eternity for someone to answer his call.
"Hello. I'm ready, call me when you get here" he whispered into the phone.
He ended the call and got back in the bed. He played sleep, in case the staff came to check on him, until he got the call. Then, he ran into the bathroom, locked the door and climbed out of the window. Being that he was on the second floor, he used the storm drain to climb down. When he finally made it down, he ran towards the gym and spotted Nicole's car parked out front with the lights out.
"Damn boy, you had me scared as hell!" spoke Nicole as Malik settled into the car. "You took so long to call me, I thought some had went wrong."
"My bad. I had to wait for the right time to leave" replied Malik.
They drove away from the group home and Malik never gave it a glance.

CHAPTER FIFTEEN

It's been weeks since Malik ran away from the group home. He decided to stay in the crib that Bo-Bo and Mack had set up. Not wanting to chance getting caught by the police, he tried his best to move around discretely. During the week, he spent time with Keisha and stayed with Nicole on the weekends because she worked during the week. Things were going fine, but Malik grew tired of being financially handicapped.

While sitting in Nicole's car at the gas station, Malik watched a silver E-Class Benz pull up to the pump on the opposite side of him. A tall, light brown skin dude stepped out with freshly done cornrows.
Malik noticed the big gold diamond necklace swinging from his neck. Malik didn't know the dude but he knew he looked like money. He looked on as Nicole finally came out the gas station. On her way back to the car, she was stopped by the light skin dude, but she continued to walk away.
Malik leaned over to the driver side window.
"You know dude or some?"
"No. He tried to holla at me, but I'm good."
"Aye, go ahead and fuck with him for me. When he come back out get his number and shit."

"Aight. I got it" replied Nicole as she started pumping the gas.

Malik rolled up the window and sat back in his seat. He watched closely as the light skin dude came back out the store, so he could remember his face. As he hoped, the dude saw Nicole and continued to holla at her. He looked on through the rearview mirror. He couldn't hear what was being said, but he could see Nicole smiling and flirting. Suddenly, she pulled out her cellphone.

'She getting the number!' Malik thought to himself.

Nicole opened the driver's door and gave dude a sexy goodbye wave as she got in. "That nigga whack as ah bitch mane!" spoke Nicole as she drove away from the gas station. He actually tried to spit that whack as game. It took all of me not to start laughing."

"What that nigga talking about?"

"He say, he wants to take me out this weekend. I got his number and told him that I was going to call him. Now, if you're going to do this, you better do it right and make it look like I ain't have nothing to do with it because I ain't got time for no dumb shit!"

"Come on shawty. You should already know that I'm not gone have shit comeback to you. I just need you to get with dude a few times and holla at Big Cee wife about them straps he left out here."

"Aight, if niggas tryna smoke and shit, we need to do it now because we don't need to draw no extra attention to ourselves while we riding dirty like this" spoke Gangsta.
Gangsta was the eldest out of the four. And having older brothers and sisters with licenses, gave him the advantage of being able to get legit rental cars.
"And don't forget that my bitch gone be in there too, so don't fuck with her" spoke Malik as they sat in the rental car smoking a blunt before they left to handle their business.
They pulled off a little bit past eleven o'clock, after Malik got the call from Nicole.
Gangsta spotted Nicole's car on Mechanicsville and followed a couple of car spaces behind her. They drove to Henrico following Nicole down Watts Lane.

Malik noticed the silver Benz pull into a driveway. Nicole parked her car right out front of the house. Gangsta drove past as if he was heading home. Malik could see Nicole walking towards the house as they drove pass. Gangsta made a U-Turn at the end of the street.
They drove back up the street riding slow with the lights out, and parked two houses away from the spot. Silently they sat, all eyes fixed on the house they were about to approach.
"Remember, we need to do this shit as quick and quietly as possible" whispered Malik. "And

no matter what! Don't kill the nigga while the bitch in there."

They got out the car and walked across the street. They crouched down when they made it to the front of the house and peeped through the windows. They crept their way to the back of the house and saw Nicole sitting at the kitchen table. The dude was walking to the table with two cups and a bottle of Grey Goose.

"BOOM!"
"Nigga, get the fuck down!" yelled Mack after he and Bo-Bo kicked open the door.
"Oh my God! Please don't hurt me, please. Please just let me go" screamed Nicole.
"WHACK!" Malik gun butted Nicole on the side of her head. "Bitch shut the fuck up! Scream again and I'ma push yo wig back" he spoke, watching the blood trickle down the side of her face.
"Check this out homeboy" spoke Malik. Either you gone give it to me or give it to God. And if you give it to God, I'ma get it anyway. So what you tryna do?"
"Mum, mum, um" mumbled dude trying to talk, but Bo-Bo had him on his knees with his .9mm River in his mouth.
"Let that nigga talk bra" spoke Gangsta holding a pump action shotgun.
Bo-Bo took his gun out dude's mouth.

"I got some work and money in a duffle bag. It's under the bed in the last room on the right. Please man, just take it. I haven't seen your face so, I don't know who you is. Please" Dude pleaded.

"Nigga get yo ass up and take us to that shit. Please try something stupid, so I can paint the wall with yo brains" spoke Malik as he pushed the dude down the hallway.

Dude dragged a duffle bag from under the bed and dropped it in front of Malik.

Gangsta hit the dude in the back of his head with the shotgun. Dude fell out from shock and fear.

Malik walked over to the night stand that sat beside the bed. He pulled open the draw, inside he found the dude's chain, a gun, and a bag of weed. He put the chain and weed in his pocket. He unzipped the duffle bag and seen the money and coke. He threw the gun in the bag and zipped it back up.

They searched the rest of the house, leaving no stone unturned. After finding nothing extra, they left.

They made it back around Fairfield and counted up everything. They ended up with sixty five thousand dollars and eighteen ounces of coke. This was the biggest lick they've ever hit.

"Mane, where the hell she at?" spoke Malik

smoking on the weed he'd gotten from dude's house. "She should've been here a minute ago."
"Aye brah." spoke Bo-Bo with a giggle. "How you gone tell us not to fuck with yo shawty, but you go and smack the shit out of her?"
The room erupted with laughter.
"Hell yeah shaw! I thought you was about to kill her for real" spoke Gangsta laughing and choking on weed smoke.
"Shid, you know I had to make that shit look good" replied Malik. "But fuck that, let's split this shit up real quick. Aye look, since I can't take that chance of being on the block in the daytime. Y'all niggas split the work and me and shawty gone split the fifteen bands that's leftover."
"Shid, that's a bet!" spoke Mack.

"Where the hell that nigga at? I'm going to fuck yo ass up when I find you boy!"

Mack looked out the door to find out who was doing all that yelling. As he peeped out the door, he saw Nicole stomping up the stairs. "Bra, that's yo ol lady. She's right here too" he whispered to Malik trying to hold back a laugh.
"Nigga, what the fuck is wrong with you?" screamed Nicole bursting through the room door.
Everyone looked at her as if she was crazy.
"Nigga, I know you hear me talking to you" she

screamed hitting Malik as he tried to walk her out of the room. "Get yo fucking hands off me! You done put your hands on me for the first and last time."

"Shawty, chill the fuck out!" yelled Malik with his arms wrapped around Nicole. "You should already know that I wasn't really tryna hurt you. But, I had to make it look real or he would've known some was up."

"You ain't have to bust my damn head wide the fuck open" spoke Nicole punching Malik in his chest. "I had to get seven stitches in my damn head because of you!"

"Let me see yo head" commanded Malik.

Nicole cocked her head to the side and lifted up some of her hair.

Malik could see the several sets of stitches.

"Oh, that ain't bad. Now, you got yourself a warrior scar" he spoke after kissing her on the forehead.

"Nigga, what you a comedian now? Get the fuck off of me" replied Nicole.

Mack, Bo-Bo, and Gangsta busted out laughing.

"What the fuck y'all laughing at? Y'all better have my shit or I'ma be whipping y'all ass next!" yelled Nicole walking back into the room.

"Aye girl, you already got yo shit split once today. You don't want it to happen again!" laughed Gangsta.

"Boy shut your big head ass up! Let me hit that blunt, y'all got my nerves fucked all up!" spoke

Nicole plopping down on the bed. 'Look at these li'l mahfuckers. They grown as ah bitch already'. she thought to herself as she felt her inner thighs getting warm from the flow of her inner juices, as Malik handed her her cut from the lick.

Malik and Nicole both had seventeen thousand, five hundred dollars each. Mack, Bo-Bo, and Gangsta took ten thousand dollars each and they split the eighteen ounces of coke evenly amongst themselves.

CHAPTER SIXTEEN

"Damn. What y'all got into last night?" asked Bo-Bo walking into the room seeing Gangsta, Mack, and Malik stretched out beside each other on the king size bed. "Y'all look fucked up!"
"Bra, you should've been here last night. We got fucked up!" spoke Mack waking up. "Ah nigga came through with some X-Pillz and we transformed out this bitch!"
"Y'all niggas popped a X-Pill! How it made y'all feel?" asked Bo-Bo excitedly.
"Shid nigga, find out for yourself. I'm about to go get some now" spoke Gangsta not even fully awake yet.

As they sat in the kitchen, they opened the oven and turned it on high. This was a way for them to stay warm so the X-Pillz would kick in full effect.
"Aye nigga, pass that blunt!" spoke Mack to Gangsta, who's been looking out the window for a minute. "You been over there cuffin for a minute shawty?"
"Shawty, that's that nigga who snitched on my brother back in the day" whispered Gangsta passing the blunt.
"Who?" asked the rest of the crew as they hurried to the window.
"That tall ass nigga right there with the

register on his hip and the chain on. My brother robbed him and his homeboys out Chesterfield back in the day and the nigga told."

"Oh yeah!" spoke Bo-Bo. "That nigga must think shit sweet out here."

They continued to watch as dude tried to holla at a group of bitches from Fairfield.

"Oh shit!" yelled Mack. "Look at bra."

"How the fuck he get out there so fast?" asked Gangsta as they saw Malik coming from the backside of the apartments.

The dude stood on the passenger side of his car, leaning over the roof, as he talked to the bitches across the street. He was so into the bitches, he ain't pay no attention to Malik walking up beside him.

"Nigga let me get this shit!" spoke Malik snatching the registered gun from dude's hip.

"Bra what's all this for?" asked dude stepping from the car.

All the bitches just stood across the street and watched.

"Let me get that chain too."

"Nah, you ain't taking my chain" said dude looking down at the shorter Malik. He figured he could overpower the li'l nigga and reached for Malik's gun.

Malik quickly grabbed dude's hand and pulled him down, at the same time, he swung his

Glock .40 and struck dude across the head. This caused dude to fall down on the sidewalk. Malik walked over top of him. "You bitch ass nigga" he slightly spoke, reaching to grab dude's chain.

Dude quickly started sitting up, but Malik stood over him and started beating him all in his face and head with the gun.

"Boy, hurry up and be out!" yelled the bitches after seeing three police cars ride down 23rd street.

Malik snatched the chain from dude's neck as he laid there unconscious on the sidewalk. He quickly walked back around the back and slid in the backdoor. Mack, Bo-Bo, and Gangsta was already waiting for him at the door.

"Here bra, put this on" spoke Mack handing Malik a clean white T-shirt.

"Hand me the strap and I'm gone catch up with y'all" spoke Gangsta going to hide the gun.

Bo-Bo, Mack, and Malik left out the backdoor and quickly made their way through the cuts, so no one would be able to make out Malik's face.

"Yeah, meet us at the store on 22nd street" spoke Malik talking to Gangsta on the phone. They went into the store and brought some Dutches and Black & Milds.

"Let's go to my crib around Mosby" spoke Mack.

"Aye bra, dude is fucked up! They don't know who it was tho' " spoke Gangsta. "You got

blood all on the strap. You know if you broke my shit, you got to buy me a new one."
"Here, take this" replied Malik handing him the chain he just took.

They made it to Mosby Court Projects and laid low at Mack's house.
"Bra, why did you have to do that shit in broad daylight like that?" asked Gangsta while they smoked and watched Bo-Bo and Mack play Madden on PS2.
"I won't even thinking about it for real, but you already know we don't tolerant that snitching shit" replied Malik.
"Yeah. But, we could've handled that shit on the low better than that" spoke Gangsta.
"Niggas already know that the law is hot around the way and niggas can't get no real money right now" Mack butted in.
"Then we can make that work in our favor" spoke Malik.
"Nigga, how the fuck is not making money gone be in our favor?" asked Gangsta.
"Brah, what the hell you talking 'bout?" asked Mack.
"Look right" spoke Malik standing up.
"Fairfield is our shit and we can do whatever the fuck we want to do! Yea, niggas gone try to talk, but they ain't gone do shit. All the old heads is chilling and getting money, they not tryna act stupid. They working out the traps and staying out the way."

"What is any of that going to do for us tho'?" asked Bo-Bo.
"Because, you know it's about to get cold. So niggas ain't gone be on the blocks, they gone get the traps jumping. That's what it do for us" spoke Malik.
"Nigga that still don't get us no money!" yelled Gangsta.
"Look, its only two ways ah nigga gets to eat dinner" spoke Malik. "Either he get a chef to cook it for him or he gone cook it himself, but ah nigga gotta cook the food in order to eat it. And I don't see a chef around here."
"What does any part of what you just said, has anything to do with what we talking about? Nigga yo ass tripping. Don't pass that nigga the blunt no more!" spoke Bo-Bo thinking the X-Pillz had Malik going crazy.
"Since niggas gone get the traps jumping" replied Malik. "We can use this time to send a message."
'If ah nigga ain't from Fairfield, if he snitching, or just in the way. They getting from around there!'
We can cause mayhem through the winter. The old heads gone let us trap with them because they gone be scared, that we might start beefing with them if they don't. So, we'll just put in work all winter and get a li'l money from the traps."
"Then what?" asked Mack. "We start killing niggas in the winter just to make a little bit of

money. Then, we go into hiding all summer because niggaz gone be too hot. That's stupid!" "No! We put in work and lay low in the winter" spoke Malik. "When we start getting at niggas, the block is going to stay hot. That's gone make the feigns go and spent money in the traps. Plus, we gone be getting money in the trap, but we only need to make enough to get us by for food and get high. Then, in the summer time, we grind hard and shine brighter because after we get all the other niggas out the way, we gone be the only ones around the hood hustling. And the streets gone talk so niggas gone get the message;
'Them Fairfield niggaz ain't playing! If you ain't from around there, don't go around there.'
And that's what I mean by we cook in the winter and eat in the summer!" explained Malik.
The rest of the crew was stunned after hearing Malik explain himself. None of them was looking at it that way. Now, they all just sat there shaking their heads in approval.
"We gone need more than the few handguns and that pump that we got." spoke Gangsta.
"Don't worry about all that. We good" replied Malik. "Gangsta, you gotta make sure you keep them 'Ave' niggas on point and out the way. We need all our niggas to be smart. We don't need anybody getting locked up because we gone need them during the summer, just in

case niggas wanna trip."

Malik and the rest of the crew finally went back around Fairfield later that night. They decided to stop by one of the many Fairfield trap houses.

As usual, the trap was packed with majority of the older niggaz from around the hood. Thick weed smoke filled the air as they made their way to the kitchen.
"What's up lil niggaz?" asked one of the older niggas.

"Aye Malik, we heard about the li'l shit that went down on Seldon Street today" spoke another older nigga. "Yo li'l ass crazy, but that was some real shit you did for the hood. You know you've been putting in a lot of work for the hood, and your name is starting to get hot. You can't keep going by Malik bra. That shit is too easy for the law to figure out who you is. So from now on, niggaz gone start calling you Mail-Man!"
"Yeah, yo li'l ass postal!" spoke another nigga. "I bet you ain't even see me watching you do that shit. You made respect from us li'l nigga. Anything y'all li'l niggaz need just holla."
"Mail-Man! You got yo stripes up now my nigga!" joked Bo-Bo.

CHAPTER SEVENTEEN

Malik got Nicole to take him to where Big Cee left all his guns. She drove him to Big Cee's house out in the county of Goochland, nearly an hour away from Richmond.

After already talking to Big Cee's wife, Nicole had the keys to the shed. Nicole flicked on the light when they walked into the shed and closed the door. Malik's eyes lit up like Christmas lights at the sight in front of him. Big Cee had so many guns and ammunition like he was funding a war. Malik started filling up his duffle bag with nothing but semiautomatic machine guns and assault rifles.

Nicole watched with a heightened since of fear. "Nigga, I don't know what you got going on and I'm not gone try and stop you. But, you better do whatever it takes to make sure that you're the one who ends up on top. Just be careful mane!" spoke Nicole.

"You don't have nothing to worry about. This shit is just for protection while my niggas trap out the spot" lied Malik. "Aye, don't ever think that you're going to be able to get away from me that easy." He joked trying to assure her that nothing was going.

Nicole dropped him back off around Fairfield.

"Y'all niggas ready for this shit?" asked Malik carefully pulling the weapons out the duffle bag and placing them on the bed.
"Fuck yeah!" Nigga where you get all this shit from?" asked Gangsta picking up the chrome carbon .308 military assault rifle.
"Let's just handle our business out here. That's all we need to be thinking about right now" replied Malik ready to put in work. "Bo-Bo, you still know how to pop cars?"
"Yea, I still got it" replied Bo-Bo.
"Aight. We gone need some stolen whips because we can't risk anything linking us or our peoples to this shit" spoke Malik.
"We need to start with them extra niggas out there on Phulpt Street and go from there.

It was a beautiful day outside. The sun was shining bright with a good breeze blowing. Kids were coming home from school and playing outside with their friends. People was sitting out on their porches and lingering around enjoying this good ole day.
Bo-Bo, Malik, Gangsta, and Mack sat parked in the alley behind the Phulpt Streets Apartments. They all dressed in black T-shirts, black skull caps, with bandannas covering their faces.
"Let's go" spoke Gangsta.
Malik and Gangsta crept around the side of the apartments.
"Oh my God!" screamed a female as she

quickly ran away.
The niggas were looking around trying to see what she was running from.
"CLAP! CLAP! CLAP! CLAP! CLAP!" were the muffled sounds from Gangsta and Malik's semiautomatics that caused the niggas and bystanders to flee and try to take cover.
Phulpt Street went intonation frenzy as people snatched up their kids, ran inside houses, and tried to shelter themselves from the hail of gunfire.
"BOOM! BOOM! BOOM! CHOP! CHOP! CHOP! CHOP! CHOP!" Gunshots broke out in rapid succession as niggas tried to run through the cut behind the apartments, only to be met by Mack's automatic shotgun and Bo-Bo's AK-47. The crew left quickly, leaving behind nothing but bodies and gun smoke.

With the projects being so hot with police. Malik and the crew stayed out in the county and away from Fairfield. They made all their moves at night. Every move they made had to be preplanned. With the amount of attention that they were bringing to Fairfield, they couldn't afford being seen or caught.
Over the past few weeks, they had established themselves as 'M.B.M' squad (Murder By any Means) and caused so much chaos around Fairfield, the residents didn't even feel safe enough to step out on their own porch.
They've been committing so many robberies,

shootings, and murders to the point, Fairfield became the main headlines on all of Richmond's news stations.

As they intended, the police constantly drove around harassing anyone they saw out on the streets, looking for a lead on a possible suspect.

CHAPTER EIGHTEEN

As the winter came to an end, the message had already spread and was being taken seriously. 'Them Fairfield niggaz ain't playing. Don't go around there if you ain't from round there!' Things gradually calmed down and the police came around less and less. This opened up some room for niggas to start back hustling on the blocks, but not without scrutiny. The more police loosened up their security, the harder Major Crimes Detectives locked their eyes on Fairfield.

Without so many extra niggas trying to catch sells, money was flowing in all directions. All Fairfield niggas made money and supported each other's hustle. Whatever drug was to be bought, the money was spent with another hustler from Fairfield. If a Fairfield nigga smoked weed, he was buying it from another Fairfield nigga. This, kept the money flowing through the hood, so every hustler ate.

"Bra, I don't know what's up with this car, but it's been circling the block all morning. I think it's the law for real" spoke Mack tryna keep Bo-Bo and Malik on point.

"Y'all, ain't dirty is it?" asked Malik as the grey Chevy Impala with tinted windows approached them slowly.

They all watched as the car got closer to them

a came to a stop. The windows swiftly began rolling down.

"Aye yo Malik, let me holla at you real quick shawty" yelled the person inside the car.

"Who that?" asked Malik while searching the car as if he had to approve of its inspection.
"Oh shit!" he whispered after realizing the person in the car.
"What's up bra?" asked Mack.
"Who the fuck is that?" asked Bo-Bo with his hand on his hip.
"Nah, it's aight. That's my people; I'll be back" replied Malik dapping them up before walking to the car.
He got in the car and they drove off.

"What's with you bra? I heard that you was out here handling yours. You know, ain't nothing wrong with putting in work. As long as that shit pays you, instead of you paying for it" spoke Wolf as he drove up I-95.
"Yeah, I'm tryna get it to pay me. I just gotta take it slow for now. You know shit is still hot out here, but fuck all that! Nigga what's up with you, how you living? It's been a minute since the last time I saw you. They say Big Cee been asking about you too. That's some fucked up shit that happened with bra!" replied Malik.
"Ain't shit change with me but the name on my I.D. After Cee got locked, I had to dip off and lay low. Me and Cee still keep in contact. He

just don't mention my name on them hotlines. Official niggas do real shit, and I'll never leave my dawg to do a bid by himself. Hell, Cee's the reason I came out to holla at you. I need you to take a ride with me and handle some business."
"When, and how long is it going to take?"
"Right now, and you'll be back in less than two days."
"Right now! What type of business you talking about?"
"I got me a nice li'l spot up top that's good for business. It's just this one nigga who's slowing up progress. He from around there so niggas rather fuck with him. And with him out the way, them niggas ain't got no other choice but to cop from me. But, if I smoke this nigga, it'll draw unwanted attention and I can't afford that right now. So, I need you to take care of this nigga and get back out of town without a problem.
"Damn mane, I'm not strapped or nothing. Plus, I don't know shit about New York."
"Don't worry about nothing. I got everything already set up for you."
Malik ran through his thoughts. "Aight bra fuck it, I'll do it."
Wolf drove the correct speed limit and obeyed all traffic laws as they made their way to New York City.

After several hours of nonstop driving, Wolf

got off the highway and pulled into a motel parking lot.

"Rest up li'l nigga because tonight we handle business. Every Friday, the nigga steps out Harlem and parlay at the poolroom on 145th street. That's where you hit him. After that, we're right back on I-95."

Without waiting for a response, Wolf left the motel room leaving Malik alone. Already exhausted from the long drive, it wasn't long before Malik drifted off to sleep.

"Knock, Knock!" were the sounds that woke Malik as Wolf knocked on the door before coming into the room.

"Mane, what time is it?" asked Malik waking up.

"Nigga, we're in a whole nother time zone up here" spoke Wolf holding a couple bags in his hand. "Get right and let me show you something."

Malik got out of bed and went into the bathroom. After taking a piss and washing his hands, he left back out the bathroom without even washing his face. "So, what's up?" he asked seeing Wolf standing with a lot of stuff on the counter.

"Check this out." Wolf reached inside of a plastic Olive Garden bag. "Do you know what this is?"

"Yeah, I know what it is" replied Malik wiping the sleep from his eyes.

"This right here is a whole key of coke. Do you

know how to make it hard?"

"Nah, I can't cook yet" replied Malik a little stunned from looking at the block of coke on the counter.

"Well, that's what I want to show you. Look, this right here is 28 grams of coke, and here I got 14 grams of baking soda. You with me?"

"Yea, I'm listening."

"Aight. So now, we gone put this shit in the Pyrex together and mix it up real good. Make sure you stir it good to even everything out." Wolf showed Malik how to turn coke into crack. "Then, take some ice cubes, bite two cubes and drop them in the pot with the coke and stir it in the water good. This helps chill the water a li'l faster. Now, take the Pyrex and sit it in a bowl of ice. As the water starts to chill, the coke will get harder. After a couple of minutes, pour the water out and there you go. That shit should hit the table like a hard ass rock." 'CLANK!' Wolf let the work drop from the pot onto the counter. "You think you can do that?"

"Yeah, but what if I fuck the shit up, then what?"

"It's hard to fuck up good coke. You can put eighteen ounces of baking soda with this." Wolf grabbed the brick of coke. "That'll leave you with some great work. If you fuck up, just add more soda. You're going to lose baking soda when you boil it, but you'll never lose coke. Coke can swim better than Michael

Phelps when in a pot so, don't worry about fucking up."
"Aight. So I do all this and sell it, but once it's all done, then what? How much you expecting me to pay you back for it?"
"In Richmond, a key goes for thirty thousand, but. I'll sell it to you for twenty. This one right here is all yours, what you do with it is on you. Niggaz showed you the game, it's up to you how you play it. I'm with you, but I'm not going to hold your hand tho'."
"Already" replied Malik understanding where Wolf was coming from.
They left the motel.

"See that nigga right there, hugged up on the car with shawty?" asked Wolf as they sat parked outside of the poolroom.
"Yeah, I see him."
"Well, that's him. Make this shit quick so we can be out."
Malik threw his hood over his head before getting out the car. As he crossed the somewhat busy street, he kept his eyes fixed on his victim. The cold New York wind cut him hard as he clutched his hoodie closer to his body. He held a .22 special revolver, wrapped in black tape (a Saturday night special) in his hoodie pocket.

His jaws began to tighten the closer he approached his target. With his victim's back facing him, Malik walked past him and quickly turned back around facing him with his .22 pointed.

The victim saw this, threw the girl in front of Malik, and took off running.

Malik chased him and shot him in his back. This caused the victim to fall face forward to the ground. He tried to crawl his way to safety, but Malik ran up on him and kicked him. He had enough strength to turn over and face Malik.

Without hesitation, Malik shot all four bullets he had left into his victim's face and hurriedly ran back to the car, as sirens could be heard in the distance.

He jumped back in the car. No words needed to be spoken as Wolf eased his way onto the highway.

They made it back to Richmond without any confrontation with the police. Wolf took Malik to Nicole's house.

"Take my number and holla at me if you need anything, but like I said, I'm not going to hold your hand. Plus, I can't risk running back and forth on that highway so, everything is on you li'l nigga."

Malik saved Wolf's number in his phone. "I got you bra. Good look on this shit too!" Malik held up the Olive Garden bag. "I'm going to be holla'n at you soon. Take your time up there." Malik dapped up Wolf and left the car. He stood and watched as Wolf drove away.

Nicole was at work so Malik chose to use this time to cook up his work. He carefully followed every step Wolf showed him. Still afraid that he was going to mess up, he cooked one ounce of coke with 14 grams of baking soda, and after doing this five separate times, he decided to just cook the last 31 ounces all at once. His wrist started to tighten the more the coke stiffened up and made it harder to whip. Inhaling the intoxicating fumes, kept him feeling as if he was going to faint. He used the back side of his forearm in an attempt to wipe the downpour of sweat from his eyes and forehead.
'Damn, I need to open up one of these windows', he thought to himself as he noticed the somewhat foggy kitchen. 'Nah, somebody might smell this shit', he thought otherwise.

Nearly two hours later, Malik stood there looking at six different sized chunks of crack laying on a sheet pan.
'Look at all this shit. Yea, I did that, Chef Boyar 'Malik'. he laughed to himself. "How in the hell I'm going to move all of this!" He spoke out loud while rubbing the waves in his hair. Malik shook himself out of the trance from looking at the work and went to get a bottle of Febreze from upstairs.
The fumes were strong all throughout the

house. Malik decided to slightly crack open the upstairs windows. He sprayed Febreze all throughout the house, cracked open the kitchen window, and began cleaning up the mess he made in the kitchen.
He divided up the work, tied it up in sandwich bags, and stashed it in the closet before going to take a shower.
"Yeah, I'm about to be that nigga!" he spoke to himself excitedly.

He stood in front of Nicole's closet wearing only a towel while trying figure out what to wear. He decided on wearing a plain white Lux Tee, blue Parish denim jeans, and a pair of Jordan Olympic #7's. He sprayed on some Playboy Vegas Cologne before grabbing some of the work from his stash spot. He threw on a grey Nike fleece hoodie and an all-black Flight jacket over that, to protect himself from the chill night winds.
After closing and locking all the windows, he put the work inside an all-black plastic bag with 'Thank You' written all over it in white letters. He sprayed a little more Febreze before he left the house, so Nicole wouldn't smell anything when she got home from work.

CHAPTER NINETEEN

As soon as he was about to step onto Seldon Street, he got a text to his phone.
"Nicole: Boo, you coming home tonight?"
"Reply: Yeah, I just left. I had to take a shower, but you can come scoop me up when you get off."
"Nicole: You want anything from the Waffle House? Cause I don't feel like cooking."
"Reply: You already know what to get."
"Nicole: Boy, you whack! I'll call you when I get round there. Be safe mane!"
"Reply: All da time!"

"Knock, knock, knock." Malik stood at the backdoor of the spot 'M.B.M.' had.
"Who is it?" yelled a female voice.
"Me!"
"Me who?"
"Mail-Man!" replied Malik.
The door was unlocked and opened before he could even finish saying his name.
"Look who finally decides to show" spoke the slim redbone, looking Malik up and down as he stepped through the doorway.
He continued walking towards the kitchen.
"What's up y'all?" he spoke to the two women in front of him.
The short, slim, brown skin one was standing in front of the oven. Her height and slim frame

made her look ten years younger than she actually was.

"Oh, so which one of them fast ass li'l bitches house you been over playa?" she asked excitedly.

"Nah, I messed around and got stuck at my cousin's house" he lied while looking at the pretty yellow bone sitting at the table.

The brown skin female caught Malik staring at the yellow bone. "Damn! Why you looking at our friend like she did some to you or she's not supposed to be here? She our company!"

This cause the yellow bone to look up at Malik that allowed him to get a clear view of her face. He looked into her almond shaped, hazel brown eyes. "Nah, I'm just tryna figure out if I know her."

"Nigga, I thought we was gone have to bank yo ass up in here!" spoke the brown skin female.

"And you don't want none of this" spoke the redbone stepping up from the side waving a box cutter.

Malik threw his hands in the air. "Whoa! I came in peace" he spoke while smiling.

"Her name is Candy. Candy, that's Mail-Man, li'l head ass" spoke the brown skin female giving Malik a wink and a head nod towards Candy. "Girl, turn the music back up."

Malik understood that she was trying to tell him to holla at Candy. He slid a chair from under the table and sat down.

"How you doing?" Asked Malik breaking her concentration from her cellphone.

"I'm fine" replied Candy.

"Candy; is that your real name or just what they call you?"

"My real name is Krystal but they call me Candy.

"Yeah, I see why they call you that."

"What's that supposed to mean?" she asked cocking her head slightly to the side. Malik took in her nude color hair flowing down the length of her shoulders, complimenting her silky yellow complexion. Big, circular, diamond earrings dangles down the side of her chiseled cheekbones.

"I'm just saying, how sweet you look over there, I can see why they call you candy."

Candy rolled her eyes at him. "Boy."

"See, why you gotta start talking that boy stuff? Girl."

"You're not grown, so you're still a boy."

"My mamah always told me, 'When you start paying bills and taking care of yourself, you're grown!'. So I'ma grown ass man."

"So you pay bills and take care of yourself? Shid, I need my bills and shit paid too! Since you got it like that."

"If you was doing the right things, you'd have your bills paid."

"I know that's right! So how old are you?"

"They say age ain't nothing but a number. So why should it matter?"

"Yeah you right, but ah bitch gotta know who she's dealing with."
"I'm fourteen" Malik lied since his birthday was in a couple of weeks.
"Damn!" she yelled with a shocked expression on her face. "You're only fourteen, that's young as hell."
"Aye, you heard what my nigga Keith Sweat said."
"What's that?" she asked, looking dumbfounded.
"Shid. I may be young, but I'm ready."
"Ah, ha, ha!" she laughed for the first time, showing her pretty whites and a gold crown on her right front tooth that compliments her smile. "That was cute."

Mack happened to come down the stairs.
"What's up nigga?" spoke Mack dapping up Malik. "Aye, I need to show you some real quick. This shit wicked bra."
"What is it?" asked Malik.
"Come on" spoke Mack walking back up the stairs.
"I'll be right back." Malik told Candy before getting up from the table.
As he reached the top of the stairs he entered the room where his crew lounged around, but the room was empty. Malik unzipped his flight jacket and pulled the black bag from the pocket of his fleece. He hit the bag on the side of the bed beside the wall.

He found Mack in one of the other rooms sitting behind the computer. "What's up?" he asked suspiciously.

"Bra, you got these bitches turned up out here" replied Mack logging on to Facebook. "You better read this shit so you'll know what's going on."

Malik waited to see what Mack was talking about. Finally, Mack showed him a list of messages to read. The first message was from Keisha, cursing somebody out for fucking Malik. Malik kept reading and saw that she was going back and forth with one of her close friends, who Malik had been fucking on the low.

"Damn shawty!" spoke Malik

"Yeah bra, you wildn with them bitches. Ain't that's like her third friend you done fucked?" Laughed Mack.

"Hell yeah. You know, you treat ah bitch how she treats herself. If she acts like a ho', you treat her like a ho'. If she acts like a lady, you treat her like a lady. She'll never stop loving you!" spoke Malik referring to one of the lessons his godmother taught him. "Aye, I'm tryna get shawty downstairs tho'!"

"Yeah that bitch bad! Bo-Bo and Gangsta already tried to holla at shawty and she gunned them down. So I don't think you gone get that jaint bra."

"Shid nigga! How much you tryna put on it?"

"Put a $100 on it then?"

"Aight, bet!" replied Malik before leaving to walk back downstairs.

"Girl, the damn club gone be closed fucking around with you" spoke Candy.
Malik stood on the last step with Mack right behind him, peeping out Candy's swag.
She was wearing some pink, grey, and white Air Max 95's. With grey denim Derion jeans, a pink and white jacket by Pink. Her slim figure and firm ass mixed with her swag and natural beauty, was enough for any man to lust over.
"What club y'all going to?" asked Malik.
"The V.I.P. LOUNGE down Shockoe bottom" replied Candy.
"That's what's up. So, when I'm gone see you again?"
"I don't know, it all depends" replied Candy before leaving out the front door.
"Ooh, give me my money nigga! I told you you won't gone get it." laughed Mack
"Fuck mane!" yelled Malik digging in his pocket. "Where Bo-Bo and Gangsta at?" he asked handing Mack five twenty dollar bills.
"Them niggas up on the Ave."
"Let's go and get them real quick."

Malik and Mack walked out the backdoor and headed towards Fairfield Avenue.
"The people pulling up on our left" spoke Malik as they stepped out the cut on Rossetta street.

"Hold up right there you two" ordered the white police officer stepping out the driver's seat. "Where are you guys headed?" he asked with a smirk as three more officers approached from behind him.
"We going home" spoke Mack.
"What do y'all have on you? Let us know now because if we have to find it, it's going to be worse" spoke the officer. Knowing that he wasn't supposed to frisk minors without the presence and permission of their guardian.
"Turn around and put your hands up."
Malik and Mack did as they were told, but neither of them answered his question. Malik's mind went blank, leaving only the thoughts of him getting locked up for leaving the group home. He was sure that the state had filed a missing person report for him.
After not finding anything on them, the officer got agitated. "Turn around" he ordered. "Give us your name and birthday" he demands. "I know who you are" he says looking at Mack. "But, what's your name boy?" he asks looking Malik up and down.
"Christopher Banks" Malik blurted out. It shocks him as he realized what he'd just said.
"How do you spell that?" asked the officer.
"C-h-r-i-s-t-o-p-h-e-r B-a-n-k-s."
"What's your date of birth?"
"Eight - fifteen, ninety - two. I'm fourteen" replied Malik innocently.

"What's your social security number?"
Malik gives him a puzzled look. "I don't know that, I'm only fourteen" he lied. He knew all his personal information from reading over all his paperwork in the group home, but he didn't want to give it to the officer because he would know that Malik gave him the wrong name. The officer gave Mack and Malik an unacceptable glance before stepping to the squad car. He walks back and takes a look at his partners. "They're clear." He looks back at Malik and Mack with anger in his eyes. "Y'all go ahead and get home. If I see either of you out here after eleven o'clock curfew, I'm taking you to juvenile."
Mack and Malik started walking away. As they waited for the police car to ride pass so they could cross the street, the police car slowed down directly in front of them and the passenger side window rolls down.
"Mack, don't forget, as soon as you turn eighteen I'm gone get you boy! I'm going to lock your ass away for life. So, you better have all your fun now while you can" yelled the officer before cruising on.
Mack had three brothers, but one was killed in a robbery, when Mack was six years old. The other two are well known killers, but the police can never get any charges on them to stick because the prosecution witnesses never live to testify. So, the history of Mack's brothers has put Mack on the police radar.

"Mane, that's some fucked up shit" spoke Malik.

"Bra, fuck that cracker! I'm not thinking about that shit he talking about" replied Mack waving off the police car. "But, who name was that you gave them?"

"I don't even know" replied Malik shaking his head. "That shit just came out. I thought I was gone be outback though for real."

"Yea, I thought they was gone lock you up too, bit you did that jaint so official."

"I know how to get them now. Shid, I'm about to come outside during the daytime too now!"

They made it to Fairfield Avenue. They came through the cut and the sounds of Yo Gotti - That's What's Up was coming from the candy lady's house. The cut was jumping like a block party. They dapped up the niggas and hugged the bitches as they walked to Gangsta and Bo-Bo, who was sitting on someone's back porch. "Damn shawty! We thought yo ass had got hemmed up or something" spoke Bo-Bo dapping up Malik.

"What's up with y'all niggas?" asked Malik.

"Shid nigga, you already know what's up with us" spoke Gangsta pulling on a blunt.

"Aye, let go to the spot. I got some shit I need to holla at y'all about" spoke Malik.

They all walked out the cut onto Newbourne street. While they were walking back to the spot, Bo-Bo punched Malik in his chest. This started a fight between the two. Mack took off on Gangsta and started a match between them too. They all fought as they made their way to the spot.

After everybody was inside the room. Malik closed the door and went to get the work he'd stashed beside the bed.
"Check it" spoke Malik reaching inside the black bag. "This is a quarter thang right here." He spoke as he threw each one of them a quarter kilo.
"Bra, how the fuck you get this?" asked Bo-Bo wide eyed.
"That don't even matter right now" replied Malik. "All that matters is that we do what we're supposed to do with it."
"What we gotta pay for this?" asked Gangsta.
"That's y'alls to do whatever y'all want and if you fuck it up that's on you too. But, I got ah nigga that's looking out so, I was thinking that we all flat foot this, bring all the money back to the table, and go big."
"Hell yea!" spoke Mack. "We can't beat this."
"How we gone do it tho'?" asked Bo-Bo.
"This how I see it" spoke Malik. "All together we got a whole brick. We need to bring at least forty stacks back to the table. Then, we take that forty stacks and flip it at."
"We got to think about the next nigga too because no matter what, we gotta have that

forty stacks" spoke Gangsta. "If one of us fuck up it's gone hurt all of us. And I don't give ah fuck, we ain't fucking this up!"
"Yeah, if ah nigga fuck up. That's on them, real talk" spoke Mack.
"Let's make it happen then" spoke Bo-Bo.
"Aight, my shawty outside. I'm gone holla at y'all niggas tomorrow" spoke Malik while dapping them up.

Malik was laid up in the bed with Nicole, eating steak and eggs with hash browns from the Waffle House. They were watching Paid And Full on DVD. Malik kept his thoughts on trying to get like Ace, from the movie.
A better life for him and his family flashed like a movie before his eyes. Seeing the smile on his sister's face brought him back to reality.
"What's wrong with you?" asked Nicole feeling Malik breathing a little hard.
"I'm full as hell." replied Malik.
They watched the movie until they fell asleep.

CHAPTER TWENTY

Malik got Nicole to drop him off on Seldon street after five o'clock in the afternoon. When they pulled up Gangsta, Bo-Bo, and Mack were standing in the middle of the street. Bo-Bo got in the front seat of someone's car who had pulled up in front of him.
"Holla at me later" spoke Malik opening the door to get out the car.
"Hold on nigga! You need to give me a kiss on the cheek or something, before you get out this damn car!" spoke Nicole.
"My bad shawty. 'Muah', you good now?" spoke Malik after giving her a kiss.
"Yea, whatever! Just be careful out here" replied Nicole slightly shaking her head.
Malik got out of the car and closed the door. Nicole sped off down the street.

"Damn bra, what you do to her?" asked Gangsta watching Nicole speed down the street.
"Shawty just be tripping" replied Malik dapping him up. "What's up with y'all niggas?" he asked dapping up Mack.
"You see what it is. Niggas ain't playing bra" replied Mack.
"Yeah, you can go ahead and hit the spot" spoke Gangsta. "We'll send some switches to the backdoor for you."

"Shid nigga! I'm out this bitch now" replied Malik stomping his feet.

"What the fuck you mean you out chea? Bra, you know them people can pull up at any given time" replied Gangsta.
"I'm good now bra. I got a name for they ass if they pull up on me" replied Malik.
"Yea, bra got off on them people like that last night" spoke Mack.
"What's up nigga?" spoke Bo-Bo dapping up Malik. "Bra, you know you pose to be in the spot. It's too early for you to be out chea."
"I just said the same shit, but bra said he good" spoke Gangsta.
"Yea, I'm good bra. I got this shit. The only thing y'all need to worry about is this competition that I'm bringing" replied Malik.
"Shid, what competition? They already know Gangsta got it" spoke Gangsta.
"Aight, let's get it then nigga" spoke Malik feeling his phone vibrate in his pocket. He pulled his phone out and saw that he had a text from Nicole.
"Nicole: You need to tighten the fuck up."
"Reply: What you talking 'bout?"
"Nicole: What, you don't want that bitch to see us or some?"
"Reply: Shawty, don't start this today."
"Nicole: Nah bitch! You started it, but I'm gone finish it."
"Reply: Aight, you got it."

"Nicole: Yea, don't worry about it."
Malik read the last text and put his phone back in his pocket.

"Mail-Man, what's up boo!" spoke one of the older bitches giving Malik a hug.
"What's up boo" replied Malik.
"Boo! Damn, you fucking with that nigga?" spoke Gangsta.
"Yeah, I thought you was feeling me!" spoke Bo-Bo.
"Nah, y'all my niggaz, but Mail-Man's my boo. Ain't that right boo?" she asked rubbing on Malik's waves. "Boy, I'll fuck the shit out yo li'l chocolate ass."
"Yeah aight! I'll be over there tonight then" replied Malik with a smile.
"See, that nigga bullshitting" spoke Gangsta.
"That nigga scared of that pussy" spoke Bo-Bo. "I'll be at yo house for real."
"I ain't fucking with y'all li'l ass today" she laughed. "Y'all something else. Mack, what's up li'l bra, you good?" she asked giving Mack a hug.
"I'm good sis." replied Mack laughing.
"Bra, she tryna give you that pussy for real shawty" spoke Bo-Bo.
"Hell yeah. You better go head and hit that jaint. And stop acting like you scared of that pussy." Spoke Gangsta looking at her walk away.
"I know, but I ain't fucking with shawty"

replied Malik.

"Don't worry about it. Watch me hit that jaint, I know she got a smoker too! Look at how she throw that jaint" spoke Bo-Bo lookin at her ass as she walked down the street.

"Damn right!" spoke Gangsta. "This nigga tripping. All he want to do is boo-love with Keisha. Oh, sucka for love ass nigga!"

"Shid." spoke Malik. "Nigga, that ain't no sucka for love shit. That's my bitch."

"Nigga, that bitch ain't yo bitch!" spoke Bo-Bo. "She probably fucking another nigga right now."

"Hell yea!" spoke Gangsta. "I bet I can fuck yo bitch."

"How much you tryna put on it?" spoke Malik. "I know you can't fuck her."

"Nigga, bet $50" spoke Bo-Bo.

"Ha, ha" laughed Bo-Bo. "All he gone do, is tell shawty not to fuck with you and take yo money."

"Yeah, ol sucka for love ass nigga" spoke Gangsta.

"Hell naw!" spoke Malik. "If she let you get on, we both can fuck that bitch! But, I know she ain't going for it."

"Aight, don't get in yo feelings over that bitch" spoke Gangsta. "If so, fuck that shit cause it ain't worth us falling out over."

"Bra, what the fuck I look like beefing with you over a bitch?" spoke Malik. "If she fuck you, knowing that you my nigga, that bitch ain't

mines anyway!"
"You gone know when I hit cause she gone be running around here like, 'Y'all seen Gangsta.'
"Ha, ha" laughed Gangsta.
"Yeah, just make sure you pay that bread when she gun yo big head ass down" spoke Malik.
"Yeah, she gone be gunning down this big ass head. She might choke" spoke Gangsta.
The rest of the crew busted out laughing.

"Aye Mail-Man, come here real quick!" yelled the redbone from the spot.
Malik walked to the spot. "What's up?" he asked giving her a hug.
"I hope you ain't doing shit tonight!" she replied with excitement.
"Nah, not for real. Why?"
"Candy want you to go out with us tonight."
"I gotta find a I.D. first."
"You don't need no I.D., we gone get you in."
"Aight. When y'all leaving?"
"She'll be here around ten o'clock. She's feeling you too! You know I talked to her about you so, all you gotta do is make sure yo game right. She's an official bitch so, just keep it real with her. And don't disappoint me!"
"You know I got you" replied Malik giving her a hug before walking back across the street.

"Nigga, I want my bread back too!" spoke Malik.
"What bread?" asked Mack.

"From that bet we made on shawty last night. Nigga, I told you I was gone get her!"

"Nigga, you ain't get that bitch! She dipped on yo ass last night" laughed Mack.

"I'm telling you bra, shawty feeling me. You gone see and I want my bread too" he replied laughing at Mack. "Let's walk on Phulpt and see what's happening."

Malik and Mack started walking towards Phulpt Street.

"Bra, look at E! She got her weight up too" spoke Mack. "I'd fuck her if she won't getting high."

"Mane, you know you'll still hit that jaint" replied Malik.

"Hell naw! You know she be tricking and shit. She might got that monkey."

"So, if you caught that jaint out on the late night and you was solo, you ain't gone try to trick with her?"

"Shid, if I was high as hell and caught her out. I ain't gone lie, I'ma creep with her" replied Mack. "She ain't fucked up. She just into too much."

"I know it. You gone catch that monkey too" laughed Malik. "Nah, you'll eat that jaint on the low tho'."

"Nigga, fuck naw! I might kiss that jaint tho'. You know, a li'l tongue action" laughed Mack.

"Yeah. Young monkey shawty!" laughed Malik.

"What up E? You back ain't you!" spoke Mack as they got closer to E.

"Oh shit! What's up y'all?" yelled E. "Y'all see me, I got my weight back now." She bent over and started shaking her ass.

Mack stepped up behind her and started grinding on her.
"You better stop." She spoke under her breath. "I damn near raised your bad ass! Where the shit at round here? These niggas out here act like they scared to sell something."
"We got it" spoke Malik. "What you looking for?"
"What y'all got? I know y'all gone lookout for y'all auntie."
"How much our auntie spending first?" asked Mack.
"I don't know yet. Y'all gotta let me test it first." She spoke leading them to her house. "I don't want no garbage."

They walked through the front door behind E. The living room was spotless.
"Don't be tracking no dirt on my floors. I just cleaned this motherfucker." She spoke walking in the backroom. She came back in the living room with her pipe and a lighter. "Y'all come on."
Mack and Malik followed her down the hallway. She went into the bathroom as they continued on towards the bedroom.
"Where y'all going?" She asked seeing them walk in to her room.

They both looked back at her confused.
"Didn't you tell us to come back here?" asked Mack.
"Yeah, come on in here" spoke E.
"What the fuck! You need help using the bathroom or some?" asked Mack.
"No. Ain't nothing wrong with this pussy! Y'all gone come in here and watch me test this shit. I don't want that smell all through my house so, come on." She spoke waving them into the bathroom.

They sat in the bathroom on the side of the tub.
"Bra, she tryna make us catch a contact in this small ass bathroom" spoke Malik with his shirt over his nose.
"Y'all ain't gone catch no damn contact off this li'l ass shit! Stop acting like y'all ain't never been around this shit before."
"We ain't never been in the bathroom with nobody smoking that shit" spoke Mack. "Bra, this the initiation! She tryna put us down and turn us into some young feigns" laughed Mack. They both laughed as they sat and watched E begin testing the work. She took the coke straight out the bag and placed it right on her pipe, without even melting it down first. The flame from the lighter was so high, it almost burned her face. She inhaled deeply and blew out a long line of smoke. She did this a couple more times and when she finished, she banged

her pipe on the end of the sink.

"It's good" spoke E, rubbing her fingers through the residue on the sink. "It got a li'l bake on it, but it's good."

"Aight, let us out this bathroom" spoke Malik. "Feel like we just got smoked out a can."

"Bra, I think I'm lightheaded" spoke Mack.

"How you think, you lightheaded?" asked Malik laughing at Mack.

"Come on, with y'all simple ass" spoke E opening the bathroom door.

They followed her out the bathroom and into her bedroom. When they reached her room, she started fiddling through her pocketbook.

"Here, give me something good for this" spoke E handing Mack $40.

"I'ma give you six for this" replied Mack putting the money in his pocket.

"Give her eight jaints for that money" Malik whispered into Mack's ear.

"Fuck naw!" replied Mack.

"Shhh! Y'all hear that?" yelled E. "Oh my God! That's them, they coming y'all."

"What the fuck you talking about?" asked Malik reaching on his hip, for a gun that isn't there. "Who coming?"

E jumped from the bed and ran to the window. "Get down! They right here, they coming y'all!" She whispered strongly as she peeped out the window.

"Shawty, what the hell you got going on?" asked Mack as he and Malik walked towards the window.

"The police, they coming. They found me y'all" spoke E frantically.

"Mane, ain't nobody even out there!" spoke Malik peeping out the window.

"Get down before they see you" spoke E trying to pull Malik from the window.

"Calm down! Yo ass geeked up right now" laughed Malik.

"Bra, and you talking about give her more" spoke Mack.

Mack and Malik stepped out into the hallway to talk.

"Bra, all this shit is profit for us" spoke Malik.

"I know, but I'm not gone just be giving shit away. I need all mines bra" replied Mack.

"Bra, we can sell wholesale work and still profit. The faster we get rid of this shit, the better. Plus, we'll get more clientele because niggas ain't breaking off like us. You feel me?"

"I feel you my nigga" replied Mack counting out the work for E.

When they walked back into the room, E had calmed down. Now, she was rubbing her fingers across the floor. Every speck she saw, she thought was a piece of coke.

"Here." Mack gave E eight dime pieces. "We gone be on Seldon."

"Okay" replied E counting her crack rocks in the palm of her hand. Her eyes grew wide after counting more than what she'd paid for.

Mack and Malik went back outside and walked

up to the Phulpt Street Apartments.

They could see a few niggas standing up against the wall as they approached. The niggas were joking and laughing until they looked up and saw Mack and Malik walking towards them. All smiles ceased.
"What's up with y'all niggas?" asked Malik approaching the group.
"Shit" they all replied grimly.
"What the money looking like out here?" asked Malik.
"Shid, niggas ain't been doing shit since all that wild been going on!" spoke one of the older niggas, who is originally from Phulpt Street. "You know, how crazy shit been out here." He spoke wide eyed at Malik to make his point.
"Ha. Yeah, I heard about all that shit" replied Malik smiling wickedly. "Shit real out here, ain't it?"
"Yea, niggas ain't tryna do nothing out here right now. Niggas ain't even tryna sell niggas no work so, this shit dry."
"Word, word" spoke Malik nodding his head.
"Aye look, I'll be right back." He dapped up the older nigga and walked off.
"Bra, them niggas was scared as ah bitch when they seen us walk up" spoke Mack as he and Malik walked back on Seldon Street.
"I saw that shit too, but fuck them niggas! I need you to let me hold an ounce until tomorrow. I'm about to go post up and catch

that money."
"Aight. But, I'm not gone let you sit round there by yourself."

"Bra, I'm good. Them niggas don't want no problems with us"replied Malik.
"Yea, but a scared nigga will kill you quicker tho' bra" spoke Mack.
"You know I'ma be strapped. Shit ain't that sweet!" replied Malik as they stepped up on the porch of the spot. "Aye, there go yo girl bra!" He giggled seeing E coming through the cut.
"Hold on real quick E. I'm coming right back out" yelled Mack.
"Hurry up dammit!" yelled E. "I got motherfuckers waiting on me."
"What's up y'all?" Malik spoke to everybody as they entered the spot.
Malik and Mack walked upstairs to their chill room. As Mack weighed out a ounce for Malik, Malik went into the Nike shoe box and grabbed Gangsta's Glock .40.
"You already know where I'm gone be bra" spoke Malik as Mack handed him the ounce of crack.
"Bra, make sure you stay on point with them niggas" spoke Mack dapping Malik up.
"Aye Mail-Man!" yelled the redbone. "Make sure you be around tonight when she come."
"Just call my phone when she pull up" replied Malik before leaving out the door.

Malik walked back on Phulpt Street. All the niggas who were just standing there before he left were gone. He walked around to the front of the apartments and there sat the older nigga.

"Where everybody went to?" asked Malik.

"Them niggas dipped off as soon as you and Mack left. They thought y'all was gone come back on some dumb shit" replied the older nigga.

"Nah, niggas won't gone fuck with them" replied Malik. "I had to go and get some more work so I can catch some of this money, since niggas just letting it pass."

"Yeah, but you know y'all got niggas shook out here" spoke the older nigga shaking his head. "Niggas don't know what y'all might do next."

"We ain't thinking about these niggas. We tryna get this paper. As long as niggas ain't getting in our way, they good."

"Shid, I feel that" spoke the older nigga nodding his head in agreement. "I ain't tryna get in y'all way, but I'm tryna eat too! These niggas ain't even tryna sell me no work because they so scared of y'all niggas."

Malik gave him a hard stare as he listened to what he had to say.

"Tomorrow, I'm gone bring you two and a quarter ounces. You do what you do and just bring me back what it cost, but don't fuck with my money shawty" spoke Malik.

"You know me, I'm not with the bullshit. I'm

that same nigga from when we was paying you to lookout for us when you was just a li'l nigga" replied the older nigga dapping up Malik.
"Ha,ha. That was a long time ago nigga!" laughed Malik.

Malik walked in the cut beside the apartments and hid his ounce and a half of crack underneath a trashcan, but kept his Glock .40 on his hip. He went back on the front street and posted up where he could keep a close eye on the trashcan. He stood and yelled at every car that drove past and spoke to every feign he saw.
After his first couple of sells he was back in the rhythm of grinding. He didn't take the time to bag up his work so, he broke off the pieces of crack according to how much they were paying. Giving the feigns more than what they paid for kept a lot of them coming back. So focused on the grind, Malik didn't even realize what time it was until his phone rung.
"Hello" spoke Malik answering his phone.
"Mail-Man, where you at?" asked the redbone. "Candy just called and she's about to pull up now."
"Aight, I'm about to come through the cut now." He replied speed walking to the trashcan. He hung up the phone and grabbed the rest of his work from underneath the trashcan before walking back to Seldon Street.

He walked through a couple of different cuts and came out on the backside of Seldon Street. Mack, Bo-Bo, and Gangsta were posted up in the cut out front of the candy lady's house. Malik walked up to the porch. "Tell them, let me get a box of Blacks." He spoke reaching in his pockets to get his money.

"Oh. So its jumping like that on Phulpt Street tho'" spoke Bo-Bo.

"I told y'all niggas it be jumping round there!" spoke Gangsta.

"Fuck yea!" spoke Malik realizing all the money in his pockets. He paid for his box of Black & Milds and stepped off the porch. While he was putting all of his money together, a burgundy Nissan Altima pulled up on Seldon Street with three females. And his phone began to ring. "Hello" he answered.

"She here now" spoke the redbone. "Where you at?"

"Yea, I see y'all. I'm coming through the cut right now."

"Aye, there go shawty from last night!" spoke Gangsta.

"Bra, that bitch is bad!" spoke Bo-Bo.

"Damn right!" spoke Malik. "I'm gone holla at y'all niggas later."

"Where you ready go?" asked Bo-Bo.

"Shid, I don't even know" replied Malik walking towards the car. "I know Mack owe me $200 when I get back tho'."

"Hell naw! For what nigga?" yelled Mack.

As Malik approached the car, the female in the passenger seat got out and hopped in the backseat. The driver's window came down. "Get in the front" spoke Candy with a sexy grin.

"Oh shit. Look at Mail-Man shawty!" yelled Gangsta, Mack, and Bo-Bo as Malik got in the car.

"What's up with you shawty?" Malik spoke to Candy as he got in the cat. He turned his head to the other women as they drove off. "How y'all doing?" he asked.

"Fine" replied the women in the backseat. They pulled up on Fourth and Front around Highland Park on the North Side of Richmond. Malik noticed a lot of people roaming in and out of this big house. Two big black dudes stood on the porch and searched everyone before they entered the house.

"What the fuck is this?" asked Malik looking at Candy.

"It's a house party" replied Candy.

"Yeah, but who house is this?" asked Malik.

"I don't know. We was invited to come" spoke Candy. "Why, you got a problem with somebody around here?"

"Nah, I'm just tryna make sure it ain't gone be no problems with these niggas."

"Bra, you good. It ain't gone be no bullshit" spoke the redbone.

"Put this jaint in yo pocketbook for me" spoke Malik passing the redbone his Glock .40. "I'll get it from you as soon as we get in."
"You don't even need that in there" spoke Candy.
"Girl, you're wasting your breath tryna tell him that. His name Mail-Man for a reason" spoke the redbone shaking her head as she put the gun inside her pocketbook.
The other two women in the backseat, sat there looking at Malik with interesting looks on their faces.
"Come on y'all" spoke Candy getting out the car. The rest of the passengers followed suit. They walked up to the house and one of the females, who sat in the backseat, whispered something into the bouncer's ear.
The bouncer looked all the women up and down before opening the front door.
Malik followed the women up the steps only to be stopped by the bouncers.
"He's with us" spoke Candy and the redbone. The bouncer looked at them and then back at Malik real hard. "Turn around and put your hands up" he ordered Malik.
Malik turned around and held his hands out to the side as the bouncer searched him. After not finding any weapons, the bouncer nodded his head towards the door for Malik to go ahead.
The music and weed smoke was jumping throughout the house. Malik followed the

women to a room in the back of the house. He got his Glock back from the redbone.

"You can just go out there" spoke the redbone. "We coming right behind you."

Malik walked back out the room and headed towards the party. When he stepped into the living room, the DJ waved him over.

"Shawty, what the hell you up to now?" asked the DJ. "This a 21 and older party so, how yo ass get in?" The DJ used to live on Phulpt Street. He ran a studio and sold weed out his house, but moved away as soon as M.B.M. started sending shots.

"My people got me in" replied Malik looking around at the many faces in the party. "You know me, I'm chilling shawty."

"Yeah, I know yo li'l ass crazy. Ain't nobody on no bullshit in here. We tryna have a good time for my nigga birthday. I heard the strippers just got here" spoke the DJ reaching inside his computer bag. "Here, take this and enjoy yourself." He handed Malik 3.5 grams of exotic weed and three Dutches.

Malik accepted the weed and started rolling up a blunt as he stood beside the DJ stand.

The strippers came into the room as soon as the DJ started playing Young Jeezy's - Gone Shake That Ass. Malik's eyes grew wide when he saw Candy walk in wearing nothing but a red two piece lingerie set.

"Yea, look at yo li'l young ass. What you know about that?" spoke the DJ after noticing the look on Malik's face. I know you got some money. You better go and feel on some of that ass."

Malik lit his blunt before moving around the thick crowd surrounding the strippers. When he got close enough to see the entertainment, the sight of the redbone doing tricks on the pole in the middle of the floor, was shocking. He just stood there and watched as they entranced the crowd.

The redbone climb all the way to the top of the pole, flipped upside down and slid down the pole headfirst, flipping back over and landing into a split while popping both of her ass cheeks as she landed on the floor.

The crowd went wild with money flying from everywhere, even the bitches threw money as the strippers had the party jumping.

Malik stood posted up against the wall watching from a distance. Candy spotted him and waved him over to her. As he made his way to her, she pointed to the chair sitting in the corner of the living room. Malik sat in the chair, Candy swayed her hips seductively from side to side as she walked towards him and sat on top of him.

Slowly, she grinded on him while looking deep into his eyes as she rubbed the back of his head. She leaned forward kissing behind his ear, licking his earlobe, slowly licking her way down the side of his neck, and lightly bit and sucked on his neck.

Malik wrapped his right arm around her waist, hoisting her down. With his left hand holding her neck, he turned to her cheek. "I might be young, but don't think you're just going to be teasing me." He whispered into her ear.
Candy sat up straight and looked at him. "So, what you want?" She asked with her arms wrapped around his shoulders.
Malik reached inside his pocket and pulled out a dollar bill. He slid the dollar in her thong and left it sitting right on her pussy.
"That mean you paying for it, right?" spoke Candy cracking a smile.
Malik looked at her. "I don't see no price tag on it, and if it got a price, it ain't worth it."
"Oh, best believe it's worth whatever price I put on it."
Malik looked at her innocently. "Then why was I taught, that it came a dime a dozen? That sounds about free to me."
"You think you got all the dimes since."
After 3 AM, Candy pulled up on Seldon Street and dropped off Malik and the redbone.
"Aight boo" spoke Candy leaning over to give Malik a hug. "I am the dime out the dozen." She whispered into his ear. 'Muah', "See you later" she spoke after kissing him on the cheek.
Malik shook his head with a smirk on his face. "That's aight shawty." He giggled before getting out the car.
"You better not fuck that up either. Not after all that hard work I put in for you nigga" spoke

the redbone as her and Malik made their way to the spot..
"Oh, I got you! Shawty gone be chasing me in a second" replied Malik.

"Let me hit that blunt" spoke Malik walking into the room where the rest of his clique sat chilling and smoking.
"Yeah, there he go! Nigga, where the fuck y'all went to?" asked Bo-Bo full of excitement.
"First, nigga let me get my bread up off you for that bet last night!" Malik spoke holding his hand out to Mack.
Mack gave Malik $200 and Malik began explaining all the details of the night with the rest of the clique as they sat and smoked.

CHAPTER TWENTY ONE

Malik woke up fully dressed and in bed with Nicole. As he rolled over, Nicole looked at him with attitude written all her face. He got out of bed, grabbed a pair of boxers, and went to take a shower. He finished his shower, put his same clothes back on, and called Gangsta to come pick him up. He walked back into Nicole's room and grabbed some work from his stash spot.

Nicole lay in bed watching TV as if Malik wasn't even there. Malik laid on the bed beside her and leaned over to kiss her.

"No. Get off me!" Spoke Nicole jerking her head away from him.

"Come here." Malik spoke softly. "What you mad for?" he asked pulling her body closer to him.

"Move! You know why I'm mad at yo black ass" she replied sliding back away from him.

"You don't know how to treat ah bitch right, always tryna showoff, and I'm getting tired of that shit!"

"Don't nobody be tryna showoff. You just be tripping" replied Malik kissing on her neck. He continued kissing on her neck and rubbed on her half naked body.

Nicole began to protest but his kisses moved lower and lower down her body, leaving behind warm trails and high anticipation. She becomes dedicated to his touch as he begins sliding down her panties.

Malik carefully lifted her legs in the air as he took her panties from around her ankles. Leaving her legs on his shoulders, he softly kissed alongside her inner thighs, making his way towards her juicy fruit. Paying close attention, he noticed her puckered lips staring at him as if they were swelling by the second. He took a second to enjoy the scene.
Nicole lay there, warm and wet from anticipation. Malik gently rubbed up her thick thighs and forcefully grabbed her by her hips and pulled her in closer, while kissing and sucking on her bellybutton, slowly making his way down to her pussy. Nicole began fainting slowly. He made his way to her throbbing clit. Flicking her clit softly with his tongue, he spreads her swollen pussy lips apart with his fingers. Immediately, her juices escaped the walls of her flesh causing his fingers to get hot. He slid his index finger inside her juice box. Then he slid his middle finger inside and stroked slowly, while still softly kissing her clit.

"Mmmm." she moans quietly.
He took out his fingers and replaced them with his tongue. Licking her swollen lips, he began fingering her clit in slow circles.
"Oh my." She moans as her body shudders.

Malik begins flicking her clit faster as he kisses her pussy lips. Softly kissing both sides separately and sliding his tongue in her pussy with every peck.

Nicole's body bucked and she grabbed ahold of Malik's head tightly with both hands. With her head dug deep into between the bed and headboard, she kept her back arched as she ground her hips and pussy into his face.

Malik took his free hand and rubbed his index finger over her pussy, making his finger slick and wet. As Nicole ground on his face, he slowly slid his wet finger inside her ass. This caused Nicole's body to jump. As he inched his finger deeper into her ass, Nicole's legs gripped tightly around his face and neck.

"Oh my, mmmm!" screamed Nicole coming close to her orgasm.

Malik's phone started ringing and he broke loose from her tight hold as her orgasm came to its peak.

"Hello" spoke Malik answering his phone. "I'm coming out now." He spoke rushing into the bathroom. He quickly wiped his face with his rag, poured some mouthwash in his mouth, and hurried downstairs without even looking at Nicole. He spit the mouthwash out on his way to the car.

"Damn nigga! What, you and shawty was rumbling or some?" asked Gangsta seeing Malik eyes nearly bloodshot red.

"Nah, I just had to get on my grown man real quick. You know, give her enough to keep her chasing ah nigga." He spoke looking at his fingers. "See, this what good pussy smell like." He spoke sliding his index finger, he stuck in Nicole's ass, under Gangsta's nose.

"Nigga, get the fuck out my face!" Replied Gangsta yanking his head away from Malik's finger. "That jaint got a li'l twang to it, too shaw."

"Ha, ha, ha, that's that grown woman shit!" laughed Malik. "I need you to stop on Phulpt Street so I can drop this work off." He spoke while making a call on his phone.

Gangsta pulled up on Phulpt Street and parked on the opposite side of the apartments.

The older Nigga got in the backseat. "What's up with y'all?" he spoke.

"Getting this bread" replied Gangsta.

"This the two and a quarter I told you I'd bring you" spoke Malik passing him the work.

"When you finish, just bring me back $2,200."

"That's what it is. So that's yo number you just called me from?"

"Yeah. Just hit that jaint whenever."

"Aight, good look shawty! I'ma hit you up as soon as I finish. I'm tryna reup with you too. Fuck these in-da-way ass niggas out here bra."

"Just hit me up" replied Malik dapping dude up before he got out the car.

They drove off and headed to the spot.

Later that night, Malik got a call from his li'l sister Jay to come to Keisha's aunt house for a second.

When Malik got there, Keisha answered the door for him. She stared him up and down before letting him in.

"Damn shawty! That's how you speak to ah nigga now?" asked Malik feeling the tension. "I can't get a hug no more?" he asked leaning in for a hug.

"Hey" Keisha replied nonchalantly before giving Malik a hug.

"Come up here Malik!" yelled Keisha's aunt.

"What's up bra?" spoke Jay giving Malik a hug before sitting back on the bed with Keisha's aunt.

"Aight, you should already know why we called you over here" spoke Keisha's aunt sitting on the bed fixing a Black&Mild.

"Nah" replied Malik playing stupid. "I came because she called" he spoke pointing at Jay.

"Well, we wanna know what's going on with you and my niece."

"What you mean what's going on with us?"

"You know. Like, do you really have feelings for her the way you say you do."

"Yes. I got strong feelings for Keisha and she should already know that. I don't know why she would even question that."

"Well, you need to start showing her that you care because you ain't doing a good job at that right now. Not only are you cheating on her, but you even cheat on her with people she be around, and that shit come right back to her. You carrying it like you just don't give ah fuck!"

"It ain't even like that. You know ah nigga still young and summer's about to come. So, I told Keisha that we shouldn't be together because I don't want to hurt her."

"You don't want to hurt her how?"

"Like I said, summer's coming up, I'm young, on the run, and I know that I'm going to be out here tryna enjoy myself and fucking other bitches."

"Well, I can understand that" spoke her aunt. "You didn't tell me that he told you all this Keisha." She spoke looking at Keisha.

Keisha just stood there with her arms folded over her chest, staring at Malik.

"Hunh." Keisha mumbled underneath her breath and calmly walked out of the room without answering the question.

Malik seen the rage on her face as she walked out and he started feeling bad about himself.

"Boy, you think yo ass is grown" spoke her aunt. "You are more mature than I thought you were, but you still got a lot to learn before you become grown" she credited. "She done caught an attitude and don't wanna talk so, I guess that's all we had wanted."

"Aight" spoke Malik leaving the room.

As he walked downstairs and towards the kitchen to leave out the backdoor, Keisha jumped up from the couch and stood in front of him, blocking his way into the kitchen.

Malik stood in front of her. "Excuse me Keisha" he spoke looking directly into her eyes.

"SMACK!" Keisha smacked him across the face so fast, if it wasn't for the pain he wouldn't have known she done it. She just stood there silently.

"Keisha, don't put yo,,,,,"

"SMACK!" She smacked him again without even letting him finish his sentence.

"Mane, don't hit me again shawty. I'm telling now" spoke Malik as he felt an irritating burn across his cheek. "Excuse me, can you move so I can leave?" He spoke still looking her in her eyes.

Keisha stood there for a moment just staring at him. Malik could see that she was beyond conversation at that moment, so he decided not to say anything. After a few seconds, she stepped to the side and allowed him to leave without uttering a word to him.

Malik left out the backdoor and headed back to the spot on Seldon Street. Rubbing his cheek, he thought that his pain couldn't come anywhere near the pain Keisha must be feeling. He felt like he was wrong, but his pride and anger wouldn't let him admit it.

He entered the spot and began walking upstairs to the room with the rest of his crew. The redbone came out of her room as he made

to the top of the stairs.
"Come on" spoke the redbone turning him around and guiding him back down the stairs.
"Where we going?"
"Candy just pulled up outside" replied the redbone.
"What's up shawty?" spoke Malik as he sat in the front seat of Candy's car.
"Hey boo!" replied Candy leaning over to kiss his cheek. "What's wrong with you tonight?" She asked feeling something different from Malik.
"Ain't nothing wrong. I just ain't know that you was coming to pick ah nigga up tonight."
"Yeah, we going out again tonight" spoke Candy.

They arrived in Downtown Richmond.
"You gone have to hold our bags until we get in" spoke Candy. "Let us do all the talking."
They walked to the front of the long line at the Candy Apple strip club. Candy and the redbone walked straight up to the bouncer at the door, Malik stood right behind them.
One of the bouncers looked Malik over. "That li'l ass nigga is y'all bodyguard?" he spoke unbelievably. "Well, he still needs to show some type of I.D. that says he's twenty one."
Candy whispered something into the redbone's ear.
"Know what, forget about it!" yelled the redbone. She turned around and walked away

from the club. On cue, Malik followed.
Malik followed her around the back of the club
and up the backstairs. As they made their way
up the stairs, Candy was halfway out the
backdoor, hurrying them to come in. Malik
continued to follow behind the redbone, who
followed behind Candy. They walked down a
narrow hallway into a room on the wall.
'Damn!' Malik thought to himself as he spotted
all the females changing outfits in the dressing
room.
The redbone led him in the club before going
back into the dressing room.
Malik sat in the chair and peeped out the
surroundings of the club. He didn't notice any
familiar faces or enemies as he eased into a
relaxed position.
"What you want to drink?" asked Candy
leaning over his shoulders.
"I don't drink for real shawty." replied Malik.
"Well, just get something anyway because you
gotta make it look like you supposed to be in
here. You over here looking like you ready to
do some you ain't got no business doing."
"Get me a couple shots of Hennessy."
"You want ice in it?"
"Nah, don't get no ice."
Candy returned with four double shots of
Hennessey. Malik took one and drunk it all at
one time.
"I thought you ain't drink" spoke Candy.
"It don't look like you was caring about that,

with all this shit you brought back."
"I was just tryna make it look good" replied
Candy sitting on his lap facing him and
wrapping her arms around his shoulders.
"Nah, I think you tryna micky me."
"Aye, you never know what the night may
bring" she spoke licking his ear.
"Oh yeah!" replied Malik looking at one of the
clubbers watching Candy. "I see you got some
real fans up in here tonight" he whispered into
her ear.
"Why you say that?"
"Don't just look right at him, but dude over
here across from me, to my left, keeps staring
at us."

Candy turned around on Malik's lap, slowly
grinding on him as she leaned back and
rubbed her hands over his head. All the while,
peeping to see who Malik was talking about.
"Oh, that's Mark broke ass!" spoke Candy
recognizing who it was. "He always tryna holla
at me, but he whack as hell. Let me go make
me some money tho'."
Candy stood and walked away. Malik sat there
with his shots of Hennessey, watching the
strippers work their magic.
While watching one of the strippers, Malik
noticed a flash of light underneath her. He
figured that it was just the lighting of the club
and thought nothing else of it. Until, she lay on
her back and began opening her legs. Every

time her legs opened, a light flashed across the face of the dude that she was dancing on. Seeing this, Malik and every other guy in the club walked over to see her dance. When he made it over there, he could see that she had some type of flashlight inside of her pussy. Noticing the crowd surrounding her, the stripper began putting on a show. She took the Black&Mild, that the dude was smoking on, and put the tip in her pussy.

'Fuck naw! Ain't no way she just did that.' Malik thought to himself as he saw the cherry on the Black&Mild lit up, as if she was smoking it with her pussy. "What the fuck!" he screamed as he watched her do it again and then she gave the Black&Mild back to the dude she was dancing with.

Money started flying. Even Malik reached into his pockets for some ones to throw at her.

As Malik turned to walk back to his seat, He caught a good look at the guy Mark who was staring at Candy. His eyes were about to pop out his head as he began to recognize the face of Michelle's ex-boyfriend, who was having sex with his li'l sister Jay. His blood boiled instantly as he pulled out his cellphone.

"Aye bra, come pick me up from the Candy Apple" he spoke into the phone as he walked back to his seat. "Bring yo nephew with you too!"

He hung up his phone and drunk another shot before sitting down. He looked around for

Candy until he spotted her a couple of feet away dancing on a nigga.

He walked over to her. "Just let sis know the next time you coming around the way and I'ma see you then" he whispered into her ear. Candy looked up at him and excused herself from the person she was dancing with. "What you mean? The club is about to close. So, where you going?" she asked as they walked back to his seat.

"I know, but I gotta go make this money real quick" replied Malik. "I'm good. My nigga about to pick me up."

"See, and I had some shit planned for you tonight."

"Aight. Give me your number and I can meet up with you when I'm finished" replied Malik pulling out his cellphone.

Malik and Gangsta sat in the club's parking lot, waiting for the club to let out.

"Pick me up from around the corner" spoke Malik getting out the car as people started exiting the strip club.

Gangsta pulled off. Malik stood there waiting until he saw the person he was waiting for. He began walking towards the crowd with only one person in his sight. When he got close enough, he put his hand on the Glock .40 that stuck out his back pocket as he came close to his target.

"Aye Mark" spoke Malik aiming the Glock .40

at Mark's head. "POP!" Malik shot Mark right in the head. "POP! POP! POP!" He shot him in his chest as his body hit the ground.
Malik ran away in the mist of the scattering crowd and got in the car.

Malik got Gangsta to drop him off around Colonial Apartments at Candy's house.
Candy answered the door and showed Malik to her bedroom.
"That shit was crazy!" spoke Candy walking to her closet. "It's good you left when you did because somebody got killed after the club closed, and police was everywhere!" It was even hard for us to leave."
"What happened?" asked Malik trying to act surprised.
"I don't know. They say somebody just started shooting in the crowd."
"Damn, that's fucked up" spoke Malik placing the Glock .40 on the bed as he took off his hoody.
"You can get comfortable" spoke Candy turning on some music. "I'm going to take a shower real quick" she spoke leaving the room.
Malik sat the Glock .40 on the nightstand as he lay back on the bed, smoking on his blunt, and waiting for Candy to finish her shower.

CHAPTER TWENTY TWO

M.B.M. sat in the room discussing how much money they all were going to put towards the reup.

"I'ma put up $15,000" spoke Gangsta, setting a standard. "And I still got some work leftover too."

"Aight. I'm gone do everything this weekend" spoke Malik after everyone agreed to put up $15,000 a piece.

That weekend.

As Nicole took a shower, Malik called Wolf to arrange a meet so he could reup.

"I got eighty jaints for you bra" he spoke into the phone. "I'ma get Nicole to bring me. Yeah I know. That's why I'm not gone tell her more than I have too. Word. I'ma call you when I'm on my way up there" he replied before hanging up the phone.

"Where in the hell you get all that?" asked Nicole walking into the room.

"What you mean where I get it?" Malik spoke softly. "I worked for it."

"Damn, boo, that a lot of money." She spoke walking closer, holding her towel around her body. "How much is it?"

"It's enough for me to do what I need to do with it" spoke Malik still counting out his

$35,000 he was putting towards the reup.
"And what you need to do with all that money."
"I need you to take me to New York so I can handle some business."
"When you have to go?"
"That's the thing, I gotta go tonight." He spoke looking at her pleadingly.
"What! Hell no." She replied walking away from the bed. "Why you ain't been say something? You gone wait 'til now to ask me."
"That's because it just came up."
"How long you got to stay up there?" she wondered. "You know I got to cover a shift at work tomorrow evening."
"We just going up there and coming right back. I can help you drive at night, but you gotta drive during the day, and we'll be back by morning."

"You are really in-da-way right now mane." She spoke shaking her head looking at the stacks of money sitting on the bed. "So, when you tryna go?"
"Shid, I'm tryna go now so we can hurry up and get back."
"Damn! Can a bitch put some thongs on or some first."
"You better put on something comfortable because we ain't getting out the car." He spoke while putting the money in a plastic bag.
"Aight nigga!" yelled Nicole putting on a pair of

boy shorts.
When they got in the car, Malik called Wolf to let him know that he was on his way. Wolf told Malik to meet him at the same motel he'd took him too. After getting the directions Malik hung up.
"Stop at McDonald's before you get on the highway" spoke Malik as Nicole turned onto Mechanicsville Turnpike.

After leaving McDonald's, Nicole put Yo Gotti's - Back 2 Da Basics album in and hit the highway. Several hours later, Malik was calling Wolf to let him know that they were pulling up at the Motel. He stepped out the car with the McDonald's bag filled with money
"KNOCK! KNOCK! KNOCK!" Malik tapped on the motel room door and waited for Wolf to let him in.
"What's up with you li'l nigga?" spoke Wolf standing behind the door letting Malik in the room.
"Shit, tryna hurry up and get back to that city" replied Malik.
"I see you been down there handling yo business" spoke Wolf as he took a quick peek at the money in the McDonald's bag. "How the fuck you move that shit so fast?"
"You know, me and my squad work together." Wolf nodded his head in approval with a big smile on his face. "That's smart li'l nigga. I like that about you. Know, a selfish nigga never last

long in this game."
"It's only right that me and my niggas eat
together."
"That's five bricks over there in that bag. The
fifth one is on me, you just keep handling your
business down there" spoke Wolf giving Malik
dap.
"Already bra! You take your time up here"
replied Malik as Wolf let him back out the
room.

"Pop the trunk." Malik spoke to Nicole as he
made it back to the car.
Nicole popped the trunk and stepped out the
car. "You driving back boo. I'm tired now"
spoke Nicole walking around to the passenger
seat.
Malik threw the bricks in the trunk and got in
the driver's seat. Feeling pressured from
driving on the highway without a license, and
five kilos of coke in the trunk made Malik start
to think about his cousin.
'Don't worry about the police. Drive like you
got a licence and you ain't got nothing to
worry about. You better worry more about
fucking up my car than the police.' His cousin
would say when he was teaching Malik how to
drive.

These thoughts calmed Malik as he drove all
the way back to Richmond anxious to hit a
kitchen. He got off the highway on the

Chesterfield County exit.

He turned to look at a sleeping Nicole. "Come on, wake up." He spoke rubbing Nicole's leg.

Nicole woke up and looked around. "What are we doing at Walmart?" she asked.

"I gotta get some shit real quick. So, come on" he spoke getting out the car.

"You swear you somebody's daddy" she spoke getting out the car and following Malik inside Walmart.

Malik grabbed a Pyrex pot and rubbed his hand across the shelf, knocking nearly all the boxes of backing soda into his cart.

"Oh yea, grab you a uniform for work while we here because we gotta go to my nigga's house." He spoke as they were passing the clothing section on their way to the register. 'Damn, I need a scale.' He thought to himself.

They left Walmart and Malik directed Nicole to one of his niggas' house in Chesterfield. When they got there, Malik's nigga left out, leaving them the house. Malik grabbed the bags from the trunk and headed straight to the kitchen. He made it to the kitchen and started placing everything on the table, prepping to cook up the five bricks.

Nicole stepped in the kitchen and saw the five bricks on the table. "Is this a kilo?" She asked holding one of the bricks in her hand.

"Yeah." Replied Malik turning on the stove.

"Well, let me get out of here" spoke Nicole

rushing back out the kitchen.

Malik began cooking up the work, the same way Wolf showed him. He opened the kitchen window to let out some of the steam. When he finished, he had seven and a half kilos sitting on the table. He cleaned up and went into the living room with Nicole as he waited for the work to dry.

'Look at her' he spoke to himself, looking at Nicole sitting up watching TV with her eyes bloodshot red from fighting her sleep.

Malik got Nicole to take him back to her house before she had to go to work. He stashed four of the bricks in her closet.

"What's this for?" asked Nicole as Malik handed her $5,000.

"It's for whatever you wanna do with it" replied Malik.

"Thank you" replied Nicole giving Malik a kiss before leaving for work.

Gangsta picked Malik up from Nicole's house later that evening.

"That's a whole brick" spoke Malik handing the rest of his crew their own kilo. "They cost $20,000 so, its every man for himself now."

Everyone's eyes grew wide as they held their brick in their hands.

"Oh, niggas is really about to shit on niggas now!" spoke Bo-Bo.

"Fuck yeah bra! Watch what I do" spoke Mack.

"Y'all niggas already talking about spending money" spoke Gangsta. "I'm telling you, y'all niggas better not fuck this up because I ain't giving ah nigga shit!"
"Yeah, we gotta be smart with this shit shawty" spoke Malik. "We still young so all we need to do is stack this bread. Fuck everything else! The bullshit can come later."
"Nah. Niggas ain't gone fuck it up, but I'ma enjoy myself tho." spoke Bo-Bo with a hard smile.
The crew started making some real money. Malik began selling weight in crack for $1,000 an ounce. By doing this and selling whole sale work to feigns, boosted his clientele and profits. He could spend $20,000 for a kilo and make at least $54,000 off of it.

Malik fell asleep early in the spot, talking on the phone with one of Keisha's friends. He woke up and stepped outside. Looking around, he saw a dude yelling at one of the young niggas. He just stood on the porch smoking his Black&Mild and watching.
"What they talking about?" asked Mack stepping out on the porch.
"I don't know" replied Malik. "I just came out here."
"Let me see what's up with these niggas" spoke Mack stepping off the porch and heading down the street.
Malik stepped off the porch and followed him.

"Aye yo, what's up with y'all?" asked Mack stepping between the argument.
"This nigga tryna tell me what to do" spoke the li'l nigga.
"What's up with you, bra?" Mack asked looking at the other dude.
"I'm tryna tell his li'l dumb ass, to stop riding up and down the street all crazy with that car" replied dude.
"Listen bra" spoke Mack. "You don't have no say so to tell him to stop doing nothing out here."
"The li'l nigga keep speeding up and down the street, making shit hot. Somebody gone call the police thinking he up to something" replied dude.
"I understand all that, but all you gotta do is come get one of us" spoke Mack pointing at Malik and himself. "Come get one of us and let us handle it because this is our shit and you don't have no place to say nothing to nobody out here brah. That's how shit gets started."
"That's my fault, you right about that" replied dude looking at Mack and Malik. "I'll let you know next time."
"To avoid all problems, that's all I'm saying bra" spoke Mack reaching to shake dude's hand.
"Aight" replied dude shaking Mack's hand. They turned and headed back up the street.

"Who car you got?" Mack asked the li'l nigga.

"It's a feign whip" replied the li'l nigga. "I gave her some work and she let me rent it."
"Take me to Moe's real quick so I can get some to eat." spoke Mack.
"Aight come on" replied the li'l nigga.
"Bra, where you going?" asked Mack seeing Malik walking away.
Malik turned around to face Mack. "I'm going back in the spot" he replied.
"You ain't riding with us?" asked Mack.
"Nah, I ain't fucking with it."
"Come on bra. You know I ain't tryna go round Creighton by myself with this li'l nigga. What if them niggas out front the store and get on some dumb shit? I'ma be outback" spoke Mack raising his hands in the air. "Come on bra, I'm hungry as ah bitch."
'I ain't tryna get in this fucking car with that li'l nigga, but I can't leave my nigga on stuck'.
Malik thought to himself. "Aight. But, we coming straight back." He spoke walking to the car.
Fairfield and Creighton are historical rivals, so it's not safe for a resident of either side to be seen in the other's project.
They drove to Moe's convenience store around Creighton Court Projects. Mack and Malik both brought themselves some Chicken & Rice.
They made it back to Fairfield with no problems and sat in the car on Seldon Street.

While sitting in the car, Bo-Bo called Mack's

phone telling him that he was on his way around Fairfield. Mack told him that they would come and pick him up so he wouldn't have to walk. Malik didn't protest the decision and the drove to Mosby Court Projects to pick Bo-Bo up from his sister's house. After picking up Bo-Bo, they stopped at the BP gas station on Mechanicsville to put more gas in the car. When the li'l nigga got out the car to get the gas, Bo-Bo got in the driver's seat.

"Who car is this?" Bo-Bo asked the li'l nigga when he got back to the driver side door.
"It's a feign jaint" replied the li'l nigga.
"Aight, get in the back" spoke Bo-Bo.
"Nah bra, I'm driving" replied the li'l nigga.
"Nigga, you gone get in the back or I'ma leave yo ass right here" spoke Bo-Bo starting up the car.
"Mane, that's crazy" spoke the li'l nigga as he got in the backseat.
Mack sat in the front seat laughing at how Bo-Bo just bucked on the li'l nigga. Bo-Bo pulled away from the gas station.

While riding down Fairfield Avenue, the li'l nigga begin panicking when he saw the law.
"Oh shit! There go the law" he spoke.
"So what nigga! You better sit yo ass back and shut up" spoke Bo-Bo.
"What the hell you getting scared for?" asked Malik looking at the li'l nigga beside him.

"Where the fuck you get this car, for real?"
"I told you, it's a junky whip. I paid her a half of gram for it" replied the li'l nigga. "I gotta take her some more later and she gone let me keep it for the day."
"Aight, I got you" spoke Bo-Bo. "I'ma pay for it for you."
"Aight, but I gotta go by myself. She don't want me bringing people to her house" replied the li'l nigga.
"Aye, let's go see what the money like around the South" spoke Bo-Bo.
"Let's go" replied Mack.
Bo-Bo drove around South Side and rode through Hill Side Court Projects on the way to Afton Projects.

As they sat at the stop sign, a police car was stopped at the stop sign opposite them. Bo-Bo waited for the police car to drive past first, before making a right turn, then a quick left turn on a side street.
Within seconds, the police was already behind them.
Don't look back, but the law behind us two deep" spoke Mack looking through the rearview mirror. "Its three of 'em now."
"Bra, I'm too dirty to pull over" spoke Bo-Bo. "If they turn them lights on, I ain't stopping."
The police turned their lights and sirens on as they followed behind them. Bo-Bo sped up.
"Turn left bra" spoke Mack.

"Don't turn left!" yelled Malik after reading the 'No Outlet' sign. "It says no outlet."
Bo-Bo quickly turned left behind an elementary school.
"I said don't turn left" spoke Malik as they drove into a dead end. "The shit said no outlet."

Bo-Bo made a U-turn and tried to drive into the police car, but the police drove in reverse while blocking his abilities to turn.
With nowhere to go, Bo-Bo slowed the car and instantly, everyone jumped out and ran.

The police cars sped off behind Bo-Bo and Mack, who ran across the elementary school playground.
Malik ran and started to hop the fence, but he saw another police car coming towards him.
"Bra, hurry up!" yelled the li'l nigga behind Malik.
Malik didn't want to chance getting locked up with the li'l nigga. "Look, run back the other way!" He yelled to the li'l nigga before climbing the fence.
When he made it across the fence, he started walking as the police car approached him from ahead.
"Get the fuck on the ground, now!" yelled the black officer as he jumped out the car.
Malik looked at the officer and seen that he was pointing his gun at him so, he took off

running.
The officer started to chase after him, but dropped his gun and had to go back and get it.
As Malik ran, another police car came down the street. When it got close, he ran across the street in front of the car and up another street, only to see police cars everywhere. He quickly searched for a place to go, but he wasn't familiar with the area so, he got down on the ground and surrendered.
It took the officer at least five seconds to reach him. The officer placed him in handcuffs and began walking him back to the police car.
As they made it to the police car, Malik saw another officer with Mack in handcuffs. They both looked at each other and shook their heads.

CHAPTER TWENTY THREE

"He's never been through this before. We can hit him soft then hit him hard" spoke the detectives.
Malik heard the detectives talking outside the interrogation room before they came in.

"Okay Mr. Matthews, let's get started" spoke the tall, white detective slamming a folder on the table in front of Malik. "We know that you and your friends are from Fairfield Court. But, what we want to know is, what were you doing robbing people in South Side last night?" asked the detective fiddling through Malik's property on the table. "Is that where you got all this money from? Well, it's too bad that we have to take it from you so soon." He spoke after hearing nothing from Malik.

Malik just sat there and looked at him.

"Mr. Matthews, You can make this a lot easier for yourself by just cooperating with us" spoke the other detective with a long nose. "This is the time for you to tell us your side of the story."
The tall detective got angry with Malik's silence. "Well, you do know that we are going to charge you for the attempted murder of Mark Jackson. Yeah, you remember that

incident you two had outside of the Candy Apple strip club a few weeks ago." He continued after seeing that Malik wasn't going to speak.

'What? That nigga ain't dead!' Malik thought to himself while still looking at the detective with a blank expression on his face.

"Yep, that's right." Spoke the tall detective.

"We know that you were in the club that night and saw the guy who was molesting your little cousin. That must've really pissed you off, huh?"

"We even got video of you leaving the club a little bit before it closed" spoke detective long nose.

"But the whole part is, we have witnesses who seen you walk up and shoot him in the head." Spoke the tall detective leaning across the table towards Malik. "You know, you are going to do some time for this carjacking, but this is going to bury you in prison.

Malik just sat there quietly as the interrogation continued.

The detectives sat there for a second waiting for Malik to say something, but he remained silent.

"Alright. You don't want to tell us your side of the story, that's fine. I understand." Spoke the tall detective.

"Give us something Malik" cried detective long

nose.

"Tell us what you know about Mail-Man" spoke the tall detective. "That's who we really want."

"That's right Malik" spoke detective long nose. "You help us get Mail-Man and we'll talk to the prosecutor about maybe getting you home when you turn eighteen."

"I highly doubt they'll say no" spoke the tall detective. " If you help us get this monster off the street, we'll make sure you are home before you're eighteen."

'I am Mail-Man, you simple mahfucker!' Malik thought to himself while continuing to remain silent.

"You don't want to help yourself, oh well" spoke the tall detective steaming hot. "Just say goodbye to your mother and family because you're never coming home to them again!" He spoke standing from his chair.

"Malik, help yourself out here" spoke detective long nose.

"You don't want to have to explain to your family why you're never coming home again."

"And just so you know" spoke the tall detective walking back towards the table. "You are still property of the state. So, we can hold you until you turn eighteen, and then charge you as an adult."

"I'll leave you my card just in case you remember anything you want to tell us" spoke detective long nose. "We're here to help you

Malik" he spoke before leaving out the room behind the tall detective.

'The last time I heard that, I was taken away from my family.' Malik spoke to himself as he remembered his sixth grade guidance counselor.

The detectives didn't have enough cause to hold Mack, so they had to release him back to his mother. They took Malik and Bo-Bo down, separately, to the Juvenile Detention Center.

"Take your clothes off" the detention staff offered to Malik.

Malik took off all of his clothes except his boxers.

"Take off your boxers, turn around, squat and cough" ordered the staff.

Malik looked at the big, black, baldhead dude and felt uncomfortable. "Bra, what type shit you on shawty?" asked Malik getting defensive.

"There's nothing up with me" replied the staff. "You have to take all of your clothes off and put this uniform on." He spoke holding up a set of clothes.

'Damn, he really gone watch ah nigga too.' Malik thought to himself while taking off his boxers.

After being fingerprinted and asked a million questions, Malik was showed to his pod. He had to take off all of his clothes again, except his boxers this time, before they locked him in a cell.

'What the fuck is this?' Malik asked himself as he entered the cell.

The cell was small. There's a blue mat lying on top of a thick concrete slab, a light on the wall, and an all-in-one metal sink, toilet and water fountain. There was nothing else beside the tan walls that were so close, he could hold his hands out and touch them both.

Malik kept walking back and forth across the floor barefooted. He still couldn't believe that he was locked up.

"Lunch time!" yelled the staff opening up the cell doors.

Malik walked out his cell and tried to hurry up and put his clothes on. All eyes were on him as the rest of the juveniles was putting their clothes on.

"Oh we got some fresh meat in this bitch!" yelled the fat kid next door to Malik.

The rest of the juveniles started laughing and whistling.

Malik looked at the fat kid and laughed. "Oh yeah." He laughed while putting on his socks. He got dressed and walked up to the fat kid.

"What's up with you shawty?" he asked.

"Ain't nun. What's."

"BOP! BOP!" Malik just started punching him in his face.

"Oh shit!" Laughs one of the juveniles.

The pod got hype watching the fight as several staff members rushed in and slammed Malik and the fat kid to the floor, breaking up the fight.

They locked them both in their cells.
"Aye yo, homeboy next door!" yelled the fat kid.
"Shawty, ain't nun to talk about!" yelled Malik.
"Look bra, I won't doing shit but playing with you." Spoke the fat kid. "Shawty, I ain't got no problems with you."
"Yeah, aight!" replied Malik.
Malik got placed on a 72 hour lockdown in his cell.
Later that afternoon.
"Matthews, they need you for court" spoke the staff opening Malik's cell.
Before being taking to the court building, Malik was handcuffed and shackled together. They walked him up the stairs from the detention center to the Courthouse. When they made it to the Courthouse, Malik was locked inside a bullpen.
Malik sat inside the bullpen looking at the women in the bullpen across from him.
"Aye Malik, what's up bra?"
"Shawty, what's up with you nigga!" yelled Malik recognizing Bo-Bo's voice. "Where you at?"
"I'm in the pen right beside you bra" replied Bo-Bo. "Oh, they got you down the Bird too (a

nickname for the detention center)?"
"Yeah. I gotta sit in fuck ass shit mane!" replied
Malik.
"What they talking about with you?"
"Bra, they talking some crazy shit shawty!"
replied Malik. "Them people funny tho' bra."

"Yeah, they kept asking me about the nigga
Mail-Man" spoke Bo-Bo. "They at bra top!"
Malik started laughing. "You know they kept
asking me the same shit bra!"
"Ha, ha, ha. Say word bra!" laughed Bo-Bo.
"Word bra!" replied Malik. "The whole time
they was talking, I was laughing in the back of
my head."

"Owens and Matthews, the Judge ready for
y'all now." Spoke the deputy coming to get
them.
"Here we go my nigga!" spoke Bo-Bo dapping
up Malik on their way into the courtroom.
When they walked in the courtroom, Malik
spotted his aunt sitting with Keisha and her
aunt. He looked at them and smiled. As he
scanned the rest of the room, he saw Nicole
sitting in the back. She blew a kiss at him as
they locked eyes.
Malik and Bo-Bo stood side by side with each
other at the podium in front the judge.
"We have Brandon Owens and Malik
Matthews. Both codefendants in the case of
Robbery, Abduction, Kidnapping, and

Carjacking." Spoke the clerk.

"Any priors?" Asked the older white judge.

"In respect to Brandon Owens." Spoke the clerk reading off a long list of prior convictions for Bo-Bo.

"In respect to Malik Matthews. He has no priors."

"So what do have?" Asked the judge.

"Your Honor. While doing routine rounds through Hill Side Court on in the South of Richmond. The arresting officers got a call over the radio, of four black males riding in a Mercedes SUV and were considered armed and dangerous" spoke the State's prosecutor.

"The officer called for backup before engaging the suspects. The suspects were asked to pull over, but instead decided to take officers on a short chase through a residential area."

"You say they were reported to have been armed and dangerous" spoke the judge. "Were there any weapons found?"

"No sir, your Honor" replied the prosecutor.

"Well, how did they become armed and dangerous?" asked the judge.

'Yea, tell us that!' Malik spoke to himself while looking at the prosecutor.

"On the night before the arrests were made. The owner of the SUV filed a report with the City Police of robbery, kidnapping, carjacking, and abduction. Stating that the suspects stopped her, pulled out a gun, forced her into the trunk of the SUV, and driving around with

her for a couple of hours before throwing her out in the street." Spoke the prosecutor. "Mr. Owens was the driver of the SUV and Mr. Matthews has been identified as the suspect with the gun in this case."
'What the fuck he talking about?' Malik spoke to himself.
The judge took a stern look at Bo-Bo and Malik. "The case will be placed on the docket for a trial date." He spoke banging his gavel. The deputies began walking Bo-Bo and Malik back to the bullpen. Malik was so mad, he didn't even look back at his family in the courtroom. As soon as they were locked inside the bullpen, their court appointed attorneys came to speak with them.
"Malik, I was appointed by the court to represent you in this case" spoke a middle aged white woman. "Is there anything you can tell me about what happened?"
"Listen, I don't know what them people is talking about" yelled Malik. "That night before I was locked up, I fell asleep talking to a girl on the phone. I don't know nothing about no robbery."
"So how did you end up in the car?"

"I was with a friend, who got a ride from a friend" replied Malik.
"Do you know the person that picked you up?"
"No. I told you, he was a friend of a friend. I don't know who he was" lied Malik.

"You say you were on the phone with a girl. Do you think this girl will come and testify to this at trial?"
"Damn right! I can even get the people who house I slept over to come too."
"Okay. They have informed me that they will be bringing additional charges up on you, but they didn't tell me what they were. The best we can do is wait and see. If I hear anything new, I'll come down to see you. I'll see you before trial Malik" spoke the attorney before leaving out the bullpen.
"Mane, this some bullshit!" Malik yelled out.

CHAPTER TWENTY FOUR

Malik has been in detention for two weeks now and spent a total of 9 days locked down in his cell for fighting.
"Matthews, you got a visit" spoke the staff opening Malik's cell.
Malik got dressed and went to the gym for his visit. When he got there, he saw his oldest sister Michelle sitting in the chair smiling at him as he walked over to her.

"Hey boo!" spoke Michelle giving Malik a hug.
"What's up with you?" he asked hugging her back.
"I'm fine. How you doing up in here?" she asked. "How is they treating you? If they treating you fucked up tell me because you know, I'll call down here and report they ass. They can try to fuck with you if they want to, I'll shut this bitch down!" She spoke with authority.
"Ha, ha, nah I'm good" replied Malik laughing hard. "This shit in-da-way tho'."
Malik and Michelle sat and talked about what was going on around Fairfield and lots more.
"Oh yeah, somebody wanted to see you too" spoke Michelle.
"Who?" asked Malik, hoping she'd say Keisha.
"Her" spoke Michelle pointing towards the gym door.

Malik looked where she was pointing and was surprised at who he seen walking towards him.

"There goes my li'l man!" yelled Malik's real mother walking towards him with her arms open for a hug.

"Hey Mah" spoke Malik with a hard smile as he gave his mother a big hug.

"Damn boy! Step back so I can get a good look at you."

Malik stepped back a couple steps so his mother could get a good look at him.

"Look at you, a handsome chocolate li'l motherfucker" she spoke with a smile. "Damn boy, you know I gave birth to yo ass in one of them uniforms. I ain't think that I'd have to come and see you in one!" She spoke pulling him in for another hug.

"Mah, I know you ain't crying" spoke Malik hearing his mother sniffling in his ear as she hugged him real tight.

"I'm so sorry baby. This is all my fault" she spoke feeling guilty and rocking side to side as she hugged him tight.

"Mah, stop crying. This ain't yo fault" spoke Malik trying to comfort her. "Mah, I'm good. I'll be out of here soon."

"I know baby, I know" she replied still hugging him tight.

"Alright, visiting hours are over with!" yelled the staff. "It's time to go!"

"Look at me, I done wasted all yo time

standing here crying" spoke Malik's mother finally letting him loose.

"Ain't it. With yo crybaby ass!" spoke Michelle.

"Its aight Mah" spoke Malik wiping her tears off her face. "Aye Krystal, what's up shawty!" He spoke seeing Candy about to walk past him. "What you doing in here?"

Candy turned and looked at him. "Hey baby! What are you doing in here? I've been looking for you too!" she spoke, giving him a hug.

Malik's mother and sister stood to the side looking Candy up and down.

"I been in here" replied Malik. "Should be out in a couple weeks tho'."

"Damn! I'm done here seeing my li'l brother" replied Candy. "You behave yourself in here and make sure you call me when you get out, boy" she spoke giving Malik a hug.

"Aight shawty" he replied as they hugged.

"Who the fuck is that?" his mother asked, looking at him crazy.

"Oh, she be around Fairfield" replied Malik.

"You must be fucking her, she calling you baby" spoke Michelle.

"Mane, I love y'all" spoke Malik giving them both hugs before they left.

The next day.

As Malik was in the pod sitting at the table by himself chilling, another one of the juveniles walked up to him.

"What's up bra?" asked the juvenile.

"What up" replied Malik.

"Shid, my nigga sent me a note from G pod and wanted me to ask you, how do you know his sister?"

"I don't know. Who is his sister?"

"The bad azz red jaint that be in visitation."

"Oh! Tell him I know her from coming around Fairfield."

"You hit that jaint shawty?" asked the juvenile with a smirk.

"Nah, I ain't hit that jaint." Malik lied, not wanting to put Candy's business out there to her brother.

"What they call you bra?"

"Mail-Man."

"I'm Lil-B" replied the juvenile dapping Malik up. "Aye, I heard about you too! They say, you and yo squad was out Fairfield getting with shit. Say, y'all was getting some bread out there too."

"That's what they saying" replied Malik.

"So what them people talking about at court?"

"They talking some dumb shit, but I ain't worried about that. I'm tryna get on that phone."

"All you gotta do is holla at the nigga who pass out clothes. Tell him to give you a blue uniform so you can use the phone tonight" spoke Lil-B putting Malik on game. "Matter fact, I got you bra." he spoke before walking off.

That night after shift change and showers, Malik was wearing a blue uniform so he would be able to use the phone.

"Hello, what's up nigga!" Malik spoke into the receiver.

"Ain't shit. Nigga, what's up with you?" spoke Gangsta.

"You already know what it is. I'm waiting on these people to do what they gone do with this bullshit."

"You know the li'l nigga right here too, with his dumb ass! Bra, niggas be smacking the shit out his ass for getting you and Bo-Bo locked. Shid, I just smacked his ass again."

"I'ma beat that li'l nigga ass whenever I catch him. How y'all living tho'? Oh yeah nigga!" yelled Malik. "You owe me $50 too! Shawty told me that you tried to holla at her."

"Damn! She got a big ass mouth mane" laughed Gangsta remembering the bet between him and Malik on Keisha. "We good out here. You need to plug me in so I can keep shit flowing until you get back out here."

"I know, but the nigga only wanna deal with me. Look tho', call Nicole and tell her to give you a pair of them shoes I just brought. You know I still got some shit out there nigga" spoke Malik, talking about the bricks he left stashed in Nicole's closet.

"Bra, you ain't heard bout shawty yet?" asked Gangsta.

"Naw, why?" asked Malik.

"Bra." Spoke Gangsta pausing for a second.

"What's up with her?" asked Malik.

"Shawty got killed in a drive by around North Side my nigga." spoke Gangsta.

"What! When the fuck was this?" yelled Malik.

"Bra, this was like a week and some change ago" replied Gangsta.

"What the fuck" Malik spoke softly while rubbing his face. "Look, I left some bread and shoes at her crib inside the closet. Check on that and if it's there, you already know what to do with it."

"I'm about to go see about that shit now."

"Take yo time out there bra. I love you my nigga" spoke Malik.

"Already. I love you too bra" replied Gangsta.

"All-da-tyme." Malik replied before hanging up the phone.

"You good bra?" asked Lil-B as Malik headed to his cell.

"Yea bra. You know, they say, when it rains it pours" replied Malik. "I'ma holla at you tomah bra. Good look too." he spoke dapping up Lil-B. Malik stripped down, walked in his cell and told the staff to close the door.

"Got damn shawty! What the fuck!" he yelled as be punched the wall and walked back and forth across the floor. "This shit crazy!"

He lay down on the mat. His anger brought

back a lot of thoughts and memories:
"The Golden Rule: Never Snitch!" "Bitches are only loyal to them dollar signs." "Never trust ah bitch and tell her your business." "See, you gone be just like your mother." "Bra, you all I got." "Don't let other people make decisions on your life." "Niggaz showed you the game, it's on you how you play it." "A selfish nigga never last long in this game." "What don't kill a boy, only makes a stronger man." "Boy, I gave birth to you in one of them uniforms." "There's consequences behind everything you do, whether good or bad." "Dont do shit unless you're ready for the consequences behind it." "Real Niggaz Stand Tall, bitch niggas sit down!"

THE END...

Characters in "A Born Victim of the Game"

Matthews:	Pregnant inmate who gives birth to a boy.
Malik:	The protagonist.
Mah:	Malik's aunt. She has custody of him
Big-Cee:	An older hustler, drug dealer and "mentor" for Malik, calling him "li'l nigga"
Jay:	Malik's li'l sister (really his cousin, Mah's daughter)
La-la:	Malik's other younger sister
Worker:	Helping Malik sell drugs
Michelle:	Malik's oldest sister
Keisha:	Malik's girl-friend (from SouthSide)
Un-named:	Keisha's aunt
Nicole:	Big-Cee's female friend
Shawty:	Anyone who's new and whose name is not known
Wolf:	Big-Cee's right hand man
Tone and Black:	Robbers who took Big-Cee's and Malik's money
Tiffany:	Big-Cee's wife

Unk:	Guy selling guns (stole them from a gunshop.)
Roe-Roe:	Malik's female friend
Un-named:	Malik's cousin (a Marine)
Un-named:	School counselor
Mark:	Michelle's ex-boy friend
Tanika:	Keisha's cousin
Mack and Bo-Bo:	Keisha's friends, later Malik's partners. Bo-Bo = Brandon Owens
Ms. Lightford:	Malik's Guardian ad litem
Gangsta:	4th member of Malik's foursome
E:	Neighborhood older woman. Tester of drug quality
Candy:	Another of Malik's girls. A stripper
Mail-man:	Malik's neighborhood name
M-B-M:	"Murder by any Means". Malik's squad

About the Author

Otis Madison is a young black man from Richmond, Virginia. He was raised in one of Richmond's six, all-black, public housing projects and learned a lot of valuable lessons through experience on their streets and the different social constructs of that society. He is now serving a 35 year sentence for 1st Degree Murder and was inspired by a fellow inmate to write a book. Not wanting to mislead or fall in line with conventional urban literature-for-profit, he is striving to bring a realistic and human overview of the urban life in a fictional setting.